M000014782

LOVE FINDS THE WAY

"Whatever happens tonight will be *your* success," he murmured. "Aren't you proud?"

Dumbly she shook her head. Tears glistened in her eyes.

He saw them and suddenly nothing could have stopped him kissing her. He bent his head and laid his lips against hers and found her as sweet as he had dreamed she would be.

For a delicious moment her soft warm breath was against his mouth and he was in Heaven.

"Gina – "

And then the moment was gone. He saw her eyes, wide and horrified and felt her pull away.

"Gina – "

"No – no, we mustn't – "

She freed herself and backed away from him.

"Please John, this cannot happen – let us forget – we *must* forget – "

"Can you forget?" he asked her, almost angrily.

"I must – I must – "

Her voice floated back to him as she fled.

THE BARBARA CARTLAND PINK COLLECTION

LOVE FINDS THE WAY

BARBARA CARTLAND

Barbaracartland.com Ltd

Copyright © 2004 by Cartland Promotions
First published on the internet in December
2004 by Barbaracartland.com
First reprint July 2007

ISBN 1-905155-02-6
ISBN 978-1-905155-02-6

The characters and situations in this book are entirely
imaginary and bear no relation to any real person or actual
happening.
This book is sold subject to the condition that it shall
not, by way of trade or otherwise, be lent, resold, hired
out or otherwise circulated without the publisher's
prior consent.
No part of this publication may be reproduced or
transmitted in any form or by any means, electronically or
mechanically, including photocopying, recording or any
information storage or retrieval, without the prior
permission in writing from the publisher.

Printed and bound in Great Britain by Cle-Print Ltd. of St
Ives, Cambridgeshire.

THE BARBARA CARTLAND PINK COLLECTION

Barbara Cartland was the most prolific bestselling author in the history of the world. She was frequently in the Guinness Book of Records for writing more books in a year than any other living author. In fact her most amazing literary feat was when her publishers asked for more Barbara Cartland romances, she doubled her output from 10 books a year to over 20 books a year, when she was 77.

She went on writing continuously at this rate for 20 years and wrote her last book at the age of 97, thus completing 400 books between the ages of 77 and 97.

Her publishers finally could not keep up with this phenomenal output, so at her death she left 160 unpublished manuscripts, something again that no other author has ever achieved.

Now the exciting news is that these 160 original unpublished Barbara Cartland books are already being published and by Barbaracartland.com exclusively on the internet, as the international web is the best possible way of reaching so many Barbara Cartland readers around the world.

The 160 books are published monthly and will be numbered in sequence.

The series is called the Pink Collection as a tribute to Barbara Cartland whose favourite colour was pink and it became very much her trademark over the years.

The Barbara Cartland Pink Collection is published only on the internet. Log on to www.barbaracartland.com to find out how you can purchase the books monthly as they are published, and take out a subscription that will ensure that all subsequent editions are delivered to you by mail order to your home.

NEW

Barbaracartland.com is proud to announce the publication of ten new Audio Books for the first time as CDs. They are favourite Barbara Cartland stories read by well-known actors and actresses and each story extends to 4 or 5 CDs. The Audio Books are as follows :

The Patient Bridegroom	The Passion and the Flower
A Challenge of Hearts	Little White Doves of Love
A Train to Love	The Prince and the Pekinese
The Unbroken Dream	A King in Love
The Cruel Count	A Sign of Love

More Audio Books will be published in the future and the above titles can be purchased by logging on to the website www.barbaracartland.com or please write to the address below.

If you do not have access to a computer, you can write for information about the Barbara Cartland Pink Collection and the Barbara Cartland Audio Books to the following address :

Barbara Cartland.com Ltd.
Camfield Place,
Hatfield,
Hertfordshire AL9 6JE
United Kingdom.
Telephone: +44 (0)1707 642629
Fax: +44 (0)1707 663041

THE LATE DAME BARBARA CARTLAND

Barbara Cartland who sadly died in May 2000 at the age of nearly 99 was the world's most famous romantic novelist who wrote 723 books in her lifetime with worldwide sales of over 1 billion copies and her books were translated into 36 different languages.

As well as romantic novels, she wrote historical biographies, 6 autobiographies, theatrical plays, books of advice on life, love, vitamins and cookery. She also found time to be a political speaker and television and radio personality.

She wrote her first book at the age of 21 and this was called Jigsaw. It became an immediate bestseller and sold 100,000 copies in hardback and was translated into 6 different languages. She wrote continuously throughout her life, writing bestsellers for an astonishing 76 years. Her books have always been immensely popular in the United States, where in 1976 her current books were at numbers 1 & 2 in the B. Dalton bestsellers list, a feat never achieved before or since by any author.

Barbara Cartland became a legend in her own lifetime and will be best remembered for her wonderful romantic novels, so loved by her millions of readers throughout the world.

Her books will always be treasured for their moral message, her pure and innocent heroines, her good looking and dashing heroes and above all her belief that the power of love is more important than anything else in everyone's life.

"Love is like a rock – it endures for ever"

Barbara Cartland

CHAPTER ONE
1880

It was almost time for HMS Liverpool to dock at Marseilles. From his view on the bridge John Chester watched the port grow nearer.

Captain Hallam clapped him on the shoulder.

"I am going to the shore office to find if there are any letters. Are you coming with me, or are you leaving me to find yours for you?"

John laughed.

"I'll be very surprised if there is a letter for me."

"Oh, come on now," Hallam said. "You must have pretty girls longing for you to return."

It was a reasonable question. John Chester was nearly thirty, well set-up, with dark brown curly hair and a twinkle in his eye that might easily capture a maiden's fancy.

"What about you?" he asked, skillfully side-stepping the question. "Did you leave any broken hearts behind?"

"If I did I just hope my wife never learns of them. She was expecting a child when I left and it may have been born by now."

"Congratulations. Your first?"

"No, the third. To tell the truth, we can't really afford any more."

"So you find children expensive?" John asked.

"Endlessly. Luckily my eldest daughter is very pretty, so she may marry a millionaire and save the family."

"I am sure you can find her one," John said with a grin. "Plenty of millionaires must travel in your ship, but I have always found that pretty girls are few and far between."

Hallam regarded him with good natured cynicism.

"That is probably because their careful fathers are keeping them well out of your path," he observed.

John roared with laughter and did not deny it.

"But I would be surprised if you really suffered from a shortage of female company, anywhere you go" Hallam added, not without a touch of envy. "There seems to be a lack of unmarried Englishmen, and I have been told many times that a man with a female at home is a man to be avoided."

"I should have thought out of sight, out of mind," John replied coolly. "Who's to know what you're doing on a trip round the Mediterranean, or, as I have been travelling, far away on distant oceans, where an Englishman is as rare as a glass of cool champagne?"

"At least you can get that here," said Hallam. "If you can afford it."

"That's the problem," John said. "I often can't. What little I have has been spent on travelling. It isn't comfortable to do that when you haven't much cash, but I prefer travelling uncomfortably to not travelling at all."

"Then how will you manage at home?" Hallam asked.

"By doing what I have always done, staying clear of women with marriage in their eyes."

"But every woman has marriage in her eyes," Hallam pointed out. "Unless she is married already and then she has a husband under her heel."

"Where no woman will ever have me," John declared firmly.

"Then you will be a bachelor all your days," Hallam predicted.

"Not at all. I know exactly the kind of girl I want and when the time comes I shall choose her – sweet-natured, kind, docile – "

"Women are not docile any more," said Hallam, aghast at this lack of realism. "They have advanced ideas. They want to be emancipated."

"That kind of girl would not suit me at all," John said. "What man wants a wife who is always arguing with him?"

"No man wants that, but it's what they get," added Hallam gloomily. "My friend, you have been away from England too long. You know nothing about *the New Woman*."

"And you do?" John asked with a grin.

"Yes, from my wife's sister, a terrifying spinster. She could have married well, but no! It's all liberation and argument. According to her, one day women will have the vote."

"Never!"

"Just as long as I'm not alive to see it. Now I must get back to my duties. We're nearly there."

As he turned away another young man who had been standing just behind them, listening to their conversation, came closer to John.

"To listen to you talk, you're a heartless devil," he observed.

"I am not heartless at all," John objected. "I am just attracted to a certain kind of lady – "

"Dolls who never speak except to say 'Oh, how wonderful you are!' and 'I'll never understand how you

3

clever men think of such things'."

John grinned.

"It makes for very engaging company."

"For a short time," Benedict expostulated. "But for life? Think of the boredom!"

"The trouble with you is that you come from a family of educated women," John responded gravely.

"It's true that my mother and sisters are extremely learned. Don't worry, old fellow. You will never be asked to meet them. Once I have told them about your ideas they wouldn't have you in the house."

"But Ben, don't they terrify you?"

"No, I grew up with women who talk good sense, so it seems natural to me. You have been spoilt by eastern women, with nothing to do but think of a man's comfort and agree with him."

"What's wrong with that?" John asked with an air of innocence.

"Oh, to blazes with you!" exclaimed Benedict. "I don't believe that you are as bad as you pretend."

"Maybe not," said John with a grin. "But almost!"

He led the way off the bridge and down to the deck, where he leaned against the ship's rail with easy grace, watching the harbour growing nearer.

Benedict Kenly, his friend who had accompanied him on part of his travels, thought that John was ungrateful as well as heartless.

He seemed oblivious to the advantages conferred by his long, lithe figure and handsome face, thought Benedict, who was sadly conscious of his own lack of height. His face was round and cherubic. Some girls were attracted by his kind heart, but they did not fall in love with him, he reflected sadly.

But John Chester, who could have his pick of pretty females, cared only for his freedom.

"Heartless," Benedict repeated.

"Let me tell you something, Ben," said John, "A man has to be a little heartless if he means to stay free of entanglements."

"Your life is full of entanglements," Benedict observed with perfect truth.

"Flirtations. I am talking about serious entanglements, the kind that lead to domesticity, like that poor devil, Captain Hallam."

"But you are going to be a Duke," Benedict noted. "You cannot stay unmarried all your life. What about your heir?"

John's eyes, as they turned on him, were so aghast that Benedict could not contain a laugh.

"What an appalling thought!" John exclaimed. "My uncle is not yet sixty. He might still marry and have an heir of his own, thus sparing me the draughty castle and the dreary inheritance."

They joined Hallam in going ashore and headed for the office where the letters of those who were travelling awaited collection.

John knew that there would be nothing for him, but it was as well to check before he and Benedict went to sample Marseilles hospitality.

But to his astonishment the man behind the desk said,

"There's been one waiting here for the last six weeks, sir."

It was not a letter, but a telegram that he handed to John. It bore his name and the name of the ship.

"It must be urgent," observed Benedict.

"I don't see how it can be. Heavens, I hope it's not that

5

girl I dined with on my last night ashore."

"Did you behave like a gentleman?"

"Of course I did. Well, one kiss." Benedict frowned and John added defensively, "She was very pretty."

He opened the telegram and became very still as he read,

"Mr. John Chester, aboard HMS Liverpool. It is with regret that we inform you that your uncle, the Duke of Chesterton, died yesterday.

It is important that you should return immediately.

James Wentworth."

John read it over twice before he could believe it. He felt he had been hit by a bombshell.

As his uncle, who had never married, was now dead, John would become the Duke, inheriting not only the title, but also the house he occupied, which had been in the family for eight hundred years.

His whole life had been turned upside down and for a moment he could not think clearly.

"Is it bad news, old man?" Benedict asked sympathetically.

"The worst," replied John, very pale. "Come on, I need a drink, urgently."

He swept his friend out of the office and into the nearest tavern and ordered a bottle of brandy in a terse voice that made the landlord scuttle. Only when he had managed to take the first drink could he recover himself enough to toss the telegram across the table at Benedict.

Benedict read it and exclaimed,

"How sad. Were you close to him, John?"

"My uncle? No, we were never on cordial terms. And now it seems I am not to be reprieved after all. I will inherit a title that I do not want and a draughty great castle that's in a very bad state of repair."

He drained his brandy in one gulp, trying to come to terms with the calamity that had fallen on him.

"A title is useless without the money to keep it up," he added. "My uncle spent his money very strangely. He became religious in his old age and filled his home with poor people who had nowhere else to go."

"I don't call that strange," commented Benedict. "I call it noble."

"You come from a family of clergy," John pointed out. "It's understandable that you sympathise, but my uncle's family never did.

"Why any man wished to spend his time helping those who were too stupid to help themselves, I cannot understand. They not only gave him a great deal of trouble and when they died he paid for their burial. Then he had to contend with their weeping relatives who did nothing for them while they were alive."

"That's a very hard thing you are saying."

"Dash it all, Benedict, don't look at me like that. I don't mean to sound callous but I have had a bad shock, and I don't know which way to turn."

"Of course," said his friend loyally, "you are saying things you don't mean."

"Yes, well, don't get sentimental about me. I don't have a soft heart. All I can see at the moment is that I have been landed in a nasty position. Goodbye my freedom, goodbye my way of life!"

"But of course you will wish to do your duty to your family now," Benedict began to say and was silenced by a look from John.

He thought his friend looked shockingly pale, like a

man in a nightmare. Which was exactly how it felt to John.

John had seen little of his uncle in recent years. He had always found other appointments to keep when his family thought it their duty to visit the Duke. He had no wish to suffer the boredom and discomfort he found at the castle.

Yet now it was his.

And he had no idea of what to do with it. Or how to solve any of the multitude of problems that were about to descend on him.

"I had planned to stop off at Marseilles for a while," he mused, "and maybe take another ship home. But now – "

"But now we must rejoin the ship," said Benedict at once.

"There is no need to spoil your trip, Ben."

"Of course I am coming with you. I will have to spend a few days with my family near Portsmouth, but then I am coming on to you. Do you think I would desert a friend when he's in trouble?"

John flashed him a grateful glance, downed another brandy and they headed back to the ship.

That night they began the journey to Portsmouth. John leaned against the railing, looking out at the choppy sea.

"My father once said Uncle Rupert was as mad as a hatter," he told Benedict.

"Because he helped the poor and oppressed?"

"Because he put them before his own family. When he inherited the title there was a reasonable amount of family money and a home which most sensible people would rejoice at owning. It had pictures, furniture, a library, in fact everything a man could want. He spent it all on his *lost sheep*.

"There were endless family squabbles and it was one

of the reasons I felt the need to travel. I could just afford one journey, but I used it to make some money, so that I could give something to my mother and sisters and have a little over to pay for the next journey. That way I managed to explore much of the Orient, while still doing my duty to them."

"What were the other reasons you wanted to travel?" Benedict asked.

John thought for a moment.

"I was looking for something," he said.

"But what?"

"I am not sure – just, something different. Something outside my own experience that would make sense of the world. I have always lived in hope and now I shall never find it. All hope is gone."

"Perhaps it isn't to be found abroad?" Benedict suggested.

"I certainly haven't found it in the places I have visited," John agreed. "Perhaps it doesn't exist."

"Of course it does," Benedict said earnestly. "It exists for everyone. But maybe you cannot just go out and find it. Perhaps you have to be ready to recognise it when it finds *you*."

"Now you are getting mystical," John reproved him.

"And you're getting tipsy, old fellow," Benedict said kindly.

"It's enough to make any man drink himself to death," John said morosely. "And whatever *it* is, I won't find it now, not in England, a country I hoped I had left behind."

He thought for a moment.

"Do you realise," he said at last, "that there is actually no need for me to go home? I might never have called at Marseilles. I could turn round and go back on the next ship."

"No, you couldn't possibly do that," Benedict said. "You are the head of the family and it is your responsibility, however much you hate it."

"I suppose you're right," John sighed. "But every word feels like chains on me. Well, there's no hope for it. Let's go to bed."

*

It was evening when they docked at Portsmouth and there was nobody on the quay to meet either of them, since nobody knew when they would be returning.

"Come to the castle and suffer with me," John pleaded.

"How can any man resist such an invitation?" Benedict exclaimed. "I will join you as soon as I have seen my family."

At last it was time to disembark. As John walked to the gangway he found a porter was already there with his luggage.

"I suppose you will want a carriage," the man said to him.

"Can you find me one with two horses?" John replied. "I live in the County of Hampshire, near the village of Little Kingsford, so it will be a long journey."

"I'll do my best," said the porter and went off.

When John disembarked a few minutes later he was pleased to see that his luggage was being loaded into a two-horse carriage.

"Goodbye old fellow," he said to Benedict. "Join me as soon as you can."

'It will be an expensive trip,' he thought as he turned towards the carriage, 'but it will be more comfortable than going by train, which usually means waiting for hours and changing several times before I finally reach the nearest station to my home.'

Suddenly he heard a voice just behind him.

"Please, please will you take me with you? I am travelling to the same part of the County as you are and no other carriage here at the moment will take me."

The voice was strong, eager and pleasant.

As John turned round in surprise he saw standing behind him a very pretty girl. She was well-dressed and was carrying a case which he would have thought would have been too heavy for her. She looked at him in a pleading way and he thought it almost impossible to refuse her request.

"Are you really going to Little Kingsford?" he asked. "It will take over two hours from here."

"I know that," she replied. "the coachmen I have asked say it is too late to take their horses so far and I don't want to stay here tonight."

"It will be a bit of a crush," John said, "but of course I will give you a lift if that is where you are going."

"I am indeed going to Little Kingsford," she answered. "I heard the man from the ship saying that was where you were going and I would be so very grateful if I can travel with you."

John smiled.

"Of course we can manage it," he said. He called the coachman and indicated for the girl's luggage to be put in with his own.

But she kept hold of her case as they began to walk and John politely tried to take it from her.

"No, thank you," she replied brightly. "I can carry it myself."

"It looks heavy."

"Oh, but I am very strong," she said cheerfully.

They reached the carriage just as all the other luggage was aboard. Without hesitation she lifted her bag and tossed it in. Then she reached into her purse and handed a shilling to the servant who had taken the rest.

"I think you should have left that to me," John murmured.

"You can tip him as well," she answered. "I don't suppose he will mind."

John hastily added his own tip and they climbed into the carriage together. As they moved off, John looked at the girl beside him. She was certainly very pretty. Her fair hair under a white straw hat was most becoming.

It was just a pity, he thought, that she spoiled her charming effect by showing so much mannish independence.

"Were you on board the ship on which I travelled?" he asked.

"No," the girl replied. "I have been staying with friends nearby, but I had to leave very suddenly."

"Not a family tragedy, I hope?"

"Oh, no. My friend has a brother who – well, he started to get a little silly about me. I could not make him take no for an answer, so I slipped away. Of course that meant I could not make proper travel arrangements, so I am going home anyhow. Then your ship came in and I heard someone saying it had come from France."

"That's right," John replied. "We called in at Marseilles, but actually I have come from the Far East. And since we are both going to Little Kingsford, I suppose we will be neighbours."

"I am going to Kingsford School as I believe they are short of teachers."

John looked at her in surprise.

"Are you a teacher?" he asked. "Somehow you don't look like a school marm."

"I am not one yet," the girl told him. "But I have had

an excellent education and I want to use it. Otherwise I will just sit about and be the daughter at home and do nothing."

"Why do nothing?" John wanted to know.

"Because that's what daughters at home do. Or they sit on charity committees, but Mama's in charge of them all so that doesn't leave me much to do. She simply will not let go of the reins and it's very exasperating when I want to be doing things."

"What sort of things?" John asked cautiously.

"Useful things. You cannot imagine how I long to be useful. I find it an intolerable waste of life to do the same chores day after day, paying visits, buying new clothes, reading ladies' periodicals."

John concealed his thought that this was an entirely proper occupation for a young female, but said diplomatically,

"That must be very boring. But I think you will find a school dull too."

"Well, I have read all the books in the library and I cannot think of anything to do except be a teacher. After all, what is life without serious activity?"

"Serious activity?" echoed John, looking at her doubtfully.

It occurred to him that, although undoubtedly pretty, she was less charming than he had first thought. Young ladies, in his view, did not speak about 'serious activity'. And if they did, a sensible man avoided them.

"But surely a woman finds her serious activity in marriage," he remarked. "And raising children is a serious activity. I dare say you will marry soon."

"No thank you," she replied as though declining a slice of bread. "The married state does not suit me."

"You have tried it?"

"No, but I have seen enough of it to know that no sensible woman would have anything to do with it."

Thoroughly taken aback, John stared at her. Young ladies were not supposed to talk like this.

"Then it's lucky for us poor devils that there aren't too many sensible women in the world," he said, trying to turn it into a joke.

"But there are some sensible women in the world," she objected. "Plenty of them, in fact."

"Then how does it happen that they get married?"

"Because the world offers them no other choice," she said. "Otherwise – "

Sensing a speech threatening him John said hastily,

"Suppose we tell each other our names?"

"I am Gina Wilton," the girl answered, offering him her hand to shake.

He took it and found his fingers almost crushed by a determined grip. He only just managed not to wince.

"And you live in Little Kingsford?"

"That's right, in the shadow of the castle."

John gave her a curious look.

"Why do you mention the castle?" he asked.

"Because the thought of it has always filled my life. I have always been able to see it from my bedroom window, the great tower rearing up against the sky. And it's a real castle too. So many places that call themselves castles are really just houses and they were only built a couple of hundred years ago.

"But Chesterton Castle was built when castles were fortresses and it has *real* turrets and battlements so that you can fire arrows at the enemy, and a *real* moat."

"Well, it isn't really a moat any more," John said. "It was filled in years ago, but you can see where it once was."

"I used to make up such stories about the castle when I was a little girl. I was a Knight in shining armour, riding forth to slay the dragon and protect the weak."

"Women were not allowed to be Knights," John said firmly.

"I was in disguise," she replied, just as firmly. "I rode the country on my trusty steed, Maximus, protecting the weak."

John privately thought that the weak would probably run for cover at the sight of this terrifying girl, but he was too much of a gentleman to say so.

"Weren't you ever the damsel in distress?" he asked.

"Pooh, who wants to do that?"

"I thought not."

"Women led terrible lives," she complained, "stuck at home all day, waiting for the men to come home from their adventures. I would rather be out there actually having the adventures. Wouldn't you?"

"Well, I do enjoy travelling," he admitted.

"Oh, yes, you said you had been to the Far East, I remember. Will you tell me all about it?"

"No," he said flatly.

"Oh! Why not?"

"Because you never let me get a word in edgeways."

"I am so sorry. I am afraid I am always doing that."

"I can imagine. I would hate to be a dragon facing you. You would talk the poor creature to death!"

She chuckled and it had a strangely pleasant sound.

"So, while I have got you quiet for a brief moment," John resumed, "allow me to introduce myself."

"Oh, yes, I didn't you give the chance to do that, did I?"

"I am surprised you noticed. You might like to know that we are going to be neighbours, because my destination is the castle."

Gina gave an exclamation.

"How exciting! Oh, please, I long to see inside it after seeing only the outside for so long. Do you think you could possibly arrange it?"

"It might be managed," John agreed.

"You could actually persuade the Duke to agree?"

"He might be open to reason."

"Really? Do you know him? The new one, I mean. John Chester. Of course I know that the old Duke died and John Chester has disappeared. There are all sorts of stories flying around about him."

"Really?" John queried. "And just what stories are they?"

"People say that he is mad and his relatives have to hide him away to avoid a scandal."

"Indeed."

"Some people say he vanished years ago and nobody knows where he is, so they are going to hire an actor to pretend to be him. Fancy that!"

"Yes, fancy. Do go on, Miss Wilton. I cannot wait to hear the rest."

"Well, the other story is that he is a criminal in some foreign prison and they are trying to get him out, but the authorities won't release him because he is so deep in villainy."

"Well, I like that one best so far. I would rather be steeped in villainy than mad."

The effect of this pronouncement was all he had hoped. Miss Wilton stared at him, her jaw dropping.

"You mean – you – ?"

"You never did allow me to speak for long enough to introduce myself. Allow me to do so now, Miss Wilton. John Chester, Duke of Chesterton. At your service."

CHAPTER TWO

She gasped.

"How *wonderful*, how marvellous for you. Surely you are very excited."

There was silence for a moment before John answered,

"Not exactly. It may sound very thrilling to you, but the last Duke had a passion for helping people who were ill or depressed and having them to stay in the castle. In a great many cases he paid their bills."

She gave a cry of delight.

"I have heard all about your uncle, Papa used to say how kind and generous he was, but how badly he was treated for all he did. He said the Duke's family were always scolding him for spending his money on strangers rather than on them."

"Really?" said John, a little awkwardly.

"Papa said he was an exceptionally kindly man."

"I suppose that is what he was," John replied. "But his family suffered because he spent so much money on strangers with the castle in a very bad state and nobody can now afford to do anything about it."

"That's what you will have to do, I suppose?"

"How can I without the money, which unfortunately, I do not have?" John asked. "I am almost certain my uncle did not leave any money. Unless some drops down from Heaven, the castle will gradually fall to the ground and disappear."

He spoke without thinking that it was an odd comment to say to a stranger. The girl gave a cry of horror.

"You cannot allow that to happen."

"I do not think I can afford to do anything else," responded John, feeling slightly indignant. "When I last visited it, I was appalled at the way it looked both inside and out. In fact, I expect the only thing I can do is to let it fall into ruins."

"But you cannot do that," Gina asserted, very firmly. "Now it is yours, you must make it look as wonderful as it looked when it was first built."

"Must I?" he demanded, feeling rather put out at the way she told him what to do without having the slightest notion of his problems.

"Of course you must. How can a Duke accept the destruction of his heritage? You have to believe that this is a duel which we cannot lose, a part of our history of which our children and grandchildren will one day be very proud."

John raised his eyebrows.

"Our children?" he echoed.

At once she realised what she had said and colour flooded her face.

"I didn't mean – oh, dear!"

"It's all right, I know what you meant," he said patiently. "You meant everyone's children and grandchildren all over the county."

"Yes, that is what I meant," she said thankfully. "I should think before I speak."

"Indeed you should," he said, remembering his grievance. "It is very easy to tell other people what to do, but when you have finished informing me of my duty, perhaps you would care to tell me how I am going to do it."

"That, of course, will take careful consideration."

"I am glad you realise it. I was beginning to think you were expecting a miracle."

"A miracle?" she echoed, staring at him. "Of course there is going to be a miracle. *We* are going to make it happen."

"*You* make it happen," he said crossly. "*I* have run out of miracles."

If she had not been sitting down she would have stamped her foot.

"Oh, don't be so – so – "

"Spineless?" he offered helpfully. "Weak-kneed? Pick any one that suits you."

"You need not think you are going to silence me like that," she said. "Because it won't work."

"I was afraid it wouldn't," he muttered.

It occurred to him that he ought to take charge of the conversation. She was charming, but like all women, she was unrealistic in her expectations and it was time that the male intellect enlightened her about life.

"Now, Miss Wilton," he said firmly, "I think you should listen to me."

He turned in order to see her better while he spoke and it was then that he was really struck by her looks. He had noticed that she was pretty, but now he realised that she was lovelier than any girl he had seen for a long time.

She was an English rose with a perfect oval face, framed by honey-coloured hair. Her fair skin was so enchanting that she seemed to be part of the sunshine itself.

Her eyes were large and blue and above them she had a pair of fierce eyebrows, of a slightly darker colour than her hair. It made her face striking and full of character.

Nor was it only the beauty of her eyes that made him

gaze at them. There was a sparkling fire within their depths. As she spoke it glowed with warmth and light, and there seemed to flow a blazing energy from her that made everything she said significant.

Of one thing he was increasingly certain.

A man might love Gina Wilton or hate her. But he would never be able to overlook her, especially when, as now, she was determined not to be overlooked.

Clearly she had set her sights on persuading him to do her bidding and he felt an increasing certainty that he was going to do it.

"Yes?" Gina asked.

"What?" he asked dreamily.

"You said I should listen to you."

"Did I?"

"Yes. Which means you have something to say."

"Have I?"

"Well surely you know whether you have or not?" she asked severely.

"Yes, yes, of course I have?"

"Well?"

"Well."

"What have you got to say to me?"

He struggled to pull himself together. He didn't want to. He wanted to stay in the glorious haze that was enveloping him, but clearly this imperious female was not going to allow it.

"I was only going to say that I cannot find the enormous amount of money which needs to be spent on the castle. Who is going to give me the fortune I need?"

He spoke in desperation and after his voice died away there was silence, except for the sound of the horses cantering along the roads.

Then Gina began to speak in a low voice which had a positive note to it,

"I am sure you can do it. I am sure you can. Where other people have run away or said it was hopeless, you will succeed."

She spoke so softly that for a moment John thought he must be thinking rather than hearing what she was saying. As he turned to look at her, he saw an expression in her eyes which he had never seen in any woman's eyes.

"Why do you say that?" he managed to gasp.

"Because I feel that I know you and I know what you are capable of," Gina answered very softly. "And I know you can do it. There is no doubt in my heart and mind that you will be successful."

John wondered at himself for listening to her. What could this girl know of the problems that faced him? And yet there was a force emanating from her that seemed to overwhelm him.

"We spoke of miracles a moment ago," he said. "Can you produce one, because that's what it will need?"

Gina who had been looking at him turned her head away. Then, in a quiet voice that he could hardly hear, she said,

"There are many ways, but perhaps the easiest for you would be if you married a great heiress."

For a moment there was silence. John was simply too thunderstruck to speak. Then he gave an awkward laugh.

"I suppose that is a practical idea, but heiresses are not easily found. I am not so conceited as to think that if I found one she would fall at my feet."

"You have a great title and I believe that rich girls always desire a title. In fact, the titled men I have met were always being run after by girls who were longing to marry an Earl, or even better a Duke. And you are a Duke, so you should be much in demand."

John stared, hardly able to believe his ears.

"You talk about me, madam, as though I am a piece of cheese that you are taking to market," he said indignantly.

"Oh, but a piece of very rare cheese," she retorted cheerfully.

"Thank you. Well, you may think me old-fashioned, but I would only marry a woman who loved me for myself and not because I have a title or a castle."

"Of course you feel that way," Gina said quickly, "and it is just what I expected you to say. But the two things go together. You may fall in love with someone who returns your feelings. Her fortune is only a wedding present and not really important to your love for each other."

"On the contrary," John replied. "I should very much dislike having to ask my wife for every penny I want to spend. To restore the castle I will need a fortune, a very large fortune, and I can assure you that no one as rich as that would want to marry a man, however important he might be, whose home was in ruins."

There was silence for a moment. Then Gina laughed.

"That is a challenge," she said. "I will find you a millionairess – "

"That is very kind of you but – "

"There is no need to be grateful because I won't just be doing it for you, but for England."

"I assure you, madam – "

"I was brought up to be very proud of being English and I cannot bear that anything so important to the country should be lost, especially as Her Majesty the Queen has made all the world very envious of us, because she has saved the Balkan principalities and arranges many marriages in Europe."

"Are you suggesting that I ask the Queen to save me?" he asked tartly, "or am I to try to save myself?"

"Oh, I know that you are laughing at me, but I am speaking seriously when I say, if you allow your wonderful castle to slip into ruins and if you don't exert yourself to save it, it is something you will regret when you are old."

She took a deep breath before adding fervently,

"You will be ashamed of having been a failure."

John stared at her, not sure that he could be hearing correctly. After what seemed a long silence he said,

"Very well, Miss Wilton. Listen to me seriously. Tomorrow I will take you round the castle, so that you will see for yourself how bad the problem is."

"Oh, I would love to see the castle. Yes, please take me round it."

"I will take great pleasure in doing so," John answered, rather grimly. "I hope it will make you stop and think, because I don't want you to go away thinking I am a coward or a fool, when actually I am being practical and sensible."

"How can you be sensible?" Gina asked. "This isn't a time for sense. It is a time for courage. Your family has fought and died for the castle. Surely you cannot be so foolish as to pass by on the other side? Are you a Chester or *aren't you?*"

"Are you really saying this to me?" John demanded.

"Oh, you think I am being impertinent."

"How very astute of you!"

"But something tells me it is what you need to hear. I think you were sent to save the castle. It is your destiny. And maybe my destiny was to be the person who revealed it to you.

"Somehow, by the help of prayer, you will find the

money and the power within yourself to rescue your heritage. Not only for yourself, but for the children who will come after you."

She spoke softly yet with so much feeling that John could only stare at her. Then as she turned away, as if she was shy of what she had said, he saw tears in her blue eyes.

He could hardly believe this was really happening. That a girl he had never met before should speak to him in such a manner was beyond belief. Yet he sensed that her words came from the very depths of her heart.

For a moment he thought he must be dreaming or perhaps she was not real.

Then, almost as if someone was forcing him to answer her, the words came from his lips.

"I will try to do what you have asked of me," he said. "But I will need help. You must promise to help me, because I cannot do it alone."

He wondered at himself, making promises to this young woman who had no right to ask for them. Yet she clearly felt that she had. And perhaps she had. Perhaps anyone who felt so passionately about something had the right to speak.

"Of course I will help you," she said. "And I have a suggestion to make which you may think is ridiculous – "

To his surprise, she seemed nervous. After her fervent confidence he had not expected it.

"You may laugh at me being so foolish," she continued, "but I wonder if my idea has come to me because perhaps Heaven itself has been listening."

John wanted to say that Heaven had better things to do than to listen to their problems. But, because he did not wish to be disagreeable, he said,

"Tell me anything you want to."

"The castle does, in some way, belong to everyone who lives around it. You and your family may live in it, but the – the idea of the castle belongs to our County. We have known it, loved it and admired it, ever since we were born. So we too have an interest in keeping it alive.

"I think you should summon everyone to the castle and let them see what a bad state it is in. Then ask for their help to restore it to its former glory."

"You mean – let strangers swarm all over my home?"

"But if they love it they won't be strangers. If they realise how much it means, not only to the County but to them personally, they would, each in their own way, offer their help."

As she finished speaking she was aware that John was staring at her in sheer astonishment.

At last he said,

"It sounds outrageous – incredible – and yet – and yet – it might work."

Gina gave a cry which seemed to ring out.

"You understand! You really understand," she exclaimed. "If they paint it and make it habitable, they could compete with each other and each room would be as beautiful and as comfortable as they could make it."

"But what would they gain from that?"

"Their names would be attached to the rooms they had restored, so that anybody visiting the castle in the future could read about them and know what they had done."

John stared at her.

Then he said cautiously,

"It is a brilliant idea. But are you quite certain people will not sneer at me? They might just laugh and say it is *your* responsibility and walk away."

"I don't think they will," she replied, "not if you talk

26

to them in the right way."

And she would know all about talking to people in the right way, he thought ironically.

"It's their heritage too," she resumed, "and they know it. They would all feel sad if it disappeared into ruins. It could never be built again and all we would have to remember it would be the pictures that people have painted of it over the years."

John was silent.

Gina could tell he was thinking it over seriously and she closed her eyes, hoping and praying.

'He must do what I want,' she thought. 'He *must*.'

John covered his eyes with one hand.

"I can't think," he said at last. "My head is spinning. At one moment your idea seems wonderful, the next moment it seems impossible."

"But you will let me come and see the castle, won't you?" she asked anxiously. "Then I will have some more ideas."

"More?" he asked in alarm.

"Oh, yes, when I see the inside I am bound to think of lots of things to do."

"You worry me more by the minute."

"My Lord Duke – "

"I think you had better call me John, and I will, if I may, call you Gina. Since we seem to have become conspirators, formality is surely inappropriate."

"But my father is a builder," she admitted, horrified.

"I am not quite sure what you mean."

"A builder's daughter cannot call a Duke by his first name."

"Nonsense, of course she can, if he wishes her to."

"But it spoils everything," she said. "You cannot be really grand if anyone can address you in a familiar manner?"

"Not anyone. Just you. And must I be grand?"

"Of course. Otherwise what becomes of your Ducal authority?"

"Do I have any?" he asked ironically. "Where has my Ducal authority been for the last hour? Crushed under your heel, that's where."

"That was only a minor aberration. I think you should resume your authority now."

"Thank you, madam. What a relief to have your permission."

"My Lord, I only meant – "

"Gina, you will address me as John or I will put you out of the carriage," he said firmly. "I am not sure I should not do so anyway."

"You wouldn't!"

"Wouldn't I?"

"John!"

"That's better."

"But – "

"Silence!"

She was quiet at once. Encouraged by the effects of his first display of Ducal authority, he added,

"This is a Duke speaking, so heed him and obey."

She giggled.

While they had been talking, the time had passed swiftly and John became aware that they had entered the County and that in a mile or so they would see the castle or what was left of it, silhouetted against the darkening sky.

"Look!" she cried. "Oh, look at it! Isn't it wonderful?"

He had never thought so, but inspired by her enthusiasm he found himself saying,

"Yes, it is."

Now the horses seemed to move a little faster, almost as if they knew their journey was at an end, John turned towards Gina.

"We are nearly there. Give me your address and I will send a conveyance for you in the morning."

She scribbled it down and gave it to him.

"I will leave this carriage at the castle," he said, "and you will carry on to your home. I will, of course, pay the reckoning for the whole journey."

"You will not," she parried at once. "I pay my own reckoning."

"Gina – "

"If you argue, I will call you 'My Lord Duke'."

That silenced him.

Now the castle was in sight. Suddenly she clasped his arm and exclaimed,

"*We will win*. Whisper it to yourself, every time you feel worried, that you will win the battle however hard it may be. I am sure, absolutely sure, in my heart and my mind that you will win!"

John took her hand in his and raised it to his lips.

"How can I fail with you to help me?"

As he spoke the carriage came to a halt at the side door of the castle.

John kissed Gina's hand once again. Then he stepped out as one of the men climbed down from the front of the carriage and started to lift his cases out of the back.

John rang the bell.

The door was answered by a familiar face. Tennison,

the butler, had been with the family for nearly twenty years.

"Good afternoon, Your Grace," he said, showing no surprise at the new Duke turning up out of the blue. Your mother is waiting for you in the drawing room."

"I will be with her directly."

He returned to the carriage door and spoke to Gina in a low voice,

"Thank you, thank you for everything you have said to me. I know that, with your help, we will win."

He kissed her hand again. Then, before she could say anything he turned and walked into the castle.

CHAPTER THREE

He was followed by the servants carrying his luggage and then the man driving the carriage turned it round for the rest of the journey.

As they drove away, Gina looked back to see if there was any sign of John and his family. But there was only the butler closing the front door.

John ran straight up the staircase to the drawing room to see his mother.

Although he had seen little of her since going on his travels, he was actually extremely fond of her.

Before her marriage she had been Lady Evelyn Gower, daughter of an Earl, and was widely held to have come down in the world, since she had secured only the younger son of a Duke. But the young Lady Evelyn had fallen in love with the Duke's younger brother and had been determined to have her way.

In her youth she had been a great beauty, reputedly with half the men in Society at her feet. It was rumoured that the Prince of Wales himself had sent her desperate love letters. Now, in her fifties, traces of that beauty still lingered in her delicate face and slim, elegant deportment.

She was a woman of eccentric ways but a lot of shrewdness. Those who thought her scatterbrained eventually learned their mistake.

John found her sitting by the fire knitting. When he walked in she gave a cry of delight and held out her arms.

"You are back!" she exclaimed. "Oh, dear boy, we missed you so much."

"I didn't get the telegram for six weeks," John replied. "But I came the moment I received it. I was so sorry, dearest Mama, that I was not here to help you with Uncle Rupert's burial."

"It was very moving," his mother said. "But he had been ill for some time after his accident, so it was a relief that he did not have to suffer any more."

"But you moved in here as I expected you to do. Are you comfortable?"

"Not at all," she replied robustly. "The castle needs a great deal doing to it." She added gloomily, "it'll probably collapse soon."

John drew in his breath, but said nothing. This was not the moment to tell his mother about Gina or what they were planning.

"Did you enjoy your time abroad?" she asked. "I thought of you so often, my darling, and was sure you were finding exciting places in foreign countries. It was so nice that you managed to send us back some money, especially when your dear Papa died."

Lord James Chester had died suddenly about a year ago, following a bad fall from a horse. But for that, he would have become the Duke, but John had always known that his father had cared little for his heritage.

He was quite content to live in a house on his brother's estate for which he paid no rent. He had no ambition or ideas as to what he should do if he became the Duke and inherited the castle.

John was sure that it had never crossed his mind for a moment that he was leaving his son with the problems that should have been his.

Lord James had been comfortably off but he had left a widow and three children younger than John. The boys went to an expensive school and the girl was at a school in London where the *debutantes* of the Season were not only instructed how to speak, sing and dance, but also how to expect the smartest and most expensive clothes to be theirs when they made their debut.

The family income could just about manage these expenses, but not the greater demands that the castle would put on it.

John looked forward with dread to the arrival of his sister, Drusilla, and his two younger brothers.

But for the moment he was determined simply to enjoy the reunion with his mother.

"I have a lot to tell you," he said to her, "but first I want to see which bedroom I am in."

Lady Evelyn smiled.

"Now that you are the Duke you have the *Royal Apartment*. Though it seems absurd to call it Royal now that it's little better than a pigsty."

"Mama!" he protested. His gloom was overcoming him again.

"You will see for yourself," said Lady Evelyn, like the Prophet of Doom.

"Why did you not stay in our own house until the castle can be repaired?"

His mother smiled.

"We moved, dearest boy, not because we wanted to be important, but simply because it was the one chance of having the walls at home repapered. In another week or so I will return."

"That is most sensible of you."

"Of course it is. But you will have to stay in this mausoleum, because you are the *Head Of The Family*."

When Lady Evelyn spoke in that portentous tone it was clear that she was thinking in capitals.

Then she dropped her tone to add,

"But if you ask me, the place is in such an appalling condition that it would be dangerous for you to stay here for long."

"Are things really as bad as that?" John asked.

"Look at this room. As you can see, the walls are peeling and two windows are damaged which have not been repaired. Your uncle put up with it, but that was for the sake of his lost sheep."

"What became of the lost sheep?"

"Oh, they are still here."

He turned sharply.

"What?"

"Well, my dear, what else was to be done with them? I could hardly turn them out into the snow."

"It's May."

"Well, it will snow in December, I dare say," she responded vaguely. "Besides, I have known snow in May."

"Mama," he said in a ragged voice, "can we keep to the point?"

"But *they* are the point. I mean they are here and they have nowhere to go. So what is to be done? The family lawyer says they must not stay in case they steal something, but since there is nothing worth stealing in the whole place it hardly seems to matter."

"Are there many of them?"

"Oh, yes – well – several. I have never really counted."

John was bereft of speech. He put the thought aside, feeling that he could not cope with the problem just now.

"Has anything happened since I have been away?" he enquired.

"Yes, I believe one of the walls at the front has fallen in, but they are waiting for you to return to see what should be done about it."

John drew in his breath, trying to believe that it was not happening.

Clearly he must have a good look at the castle before he could do anything else.

"Go to bed, my dear," suggested his mother. "I will have some refreshments sent up to the Royal Apartment."

"Mama, I wish you wouldn't speak of it like that. The very idea of me in a Royal Apartment is absurd. Why not just say 'your room'?"

"Because you are the Duke of Chesterton and it is incumbent on you to keep up the proper style."

"Even though I sleep in a pigsty, according to you?"

"Even a sty can have style," said Lady Evelyn unanswerably. "Never forget that you are the Duke and that is a fine position to be in!"

"Why Mama, I do believe you are overcome with Ducal importance. I thought you didn't care for it."

"Don't be silly. How can anyone not care for a coronet?"

"But you could have worn one if you had married my uncle. Everyone knows that."

"I know," she agreed with a sigh. "But I happened to fall in love with your Papa. It was *most* inconvenient."

"Was Uncle Rupert in love with you?"

"Oh, yes. He and your father fought a duel. It was very exciting."

"You didn't worry in case one of them was killed?" John asked, fascinated.

"Of course not. They only fought with their fists, so I suppose strictly speaking it wasn't a duel, but that was what we all called it."

"What happened?"

"Your Papa aimed a punch at Rupert and missed. Then Rupert punched back and hit him more by luck than judgement. Papa staggered back and tripped over a duck that had wandered from the pond nearby, which made him sit down very suddenly. Rupert declared that honour was satisfied and that was that. He was best man at our wedding. He and your Papa were very fond of each other."

"I'll wager you enjoyed every minute of it," John said with a grin.

"Certainly I did. There wasn't another girl in London who had such turmoil over her. The others were green with envy."

"Good for you, Mama!"

"Well, these things are sent to us to be enjoyed. I don't see what other purpose they could have."

"Did Uncle Rupert ever get over you?"

"He said not. According to him he remained unmarried so that my son could inherit his title."

"No?"

"His exact words were, 'then you and I will have a share in the next Duke, Evelyn, and that is all the comfort I can have on this earth'."

"He actually said that?" John demanded, revolted.

"I am afraid he did. I don't know how I kept a straight face."

John roared with laughter.

"And he actually meant it?" he quizzed, when he had

recovered himself enough to speak.

"Oh, my dear, of course not. Once he had recovered from his so-called passion for me, he enjoyed being a bachelor, and it was his way of getting out of having to marry. But it sounded very affecting and of course it was very flattering for me. Most enjoyable.

"In the end he was glad I wasn't around to interfere with his plans to fill the castle with his strange friends. You will meet them tomorrow."

"Yes, I suppose I must."

"And you will also meet Ambrose Faber."

An odd note in her voice that he had not heard before, made John turn and ask suspiciously,

"Tell me the worst, Mama. Just who is Ambrose Faber?"

"Who is Ambrose Faber?" Lady Evelyn echoed. "My dear boy, how can you be so absurd as not to know that the Fabers are related to us? Somewhat distantly, it's true, but Rupert believed we should help poor relations."

"You mean he is a lost sheep?"

"Certainly not. He is a very educated and cultured man and Rupert engaged him as his secretary. You will find him very useful."

"What will I do with a secretary?" John demanded. "Ask him to take notes about which part of the castle falls down first?"

He sighed.

"Ah well, it's too much to think about now. I'll go up to my room – "

"You mean the Royal Apartment," she corrected him gently. "Remember your Ducal dignity."

"For Heavens sake, Mama! You are as bad as Gina."

"And who is Gina?"

"Miss Gina Wilton is a young lady I met at Portsmouth. She lives near here and I conveyed her in the carriage for part of the journey."

"Is she pretty?" asked Lady Evelyn.

"She is a school marm," John said firmly. "And extremely bossy."

"Oh, dear! Then she wouldn't suit you, I do see that."

"Suit me?" John echoed, appalled. "Let me assure you Mama, that nothing is further from my mind than to ally myself with a young woman who cannot open her mouth without giving orders about something that is none of her concern."

"She sounds very strong-minded," Lady Evelyn remarked dubiously. "Perhaps she is one of those *New Women* we hear about these days with ideas about emancipation."

"That sounds just like her."

"What a dreadful female. Never mind, my dear, you showed her courtesy and now you need not see her again, which I am sure must be a great relief to you."

He hesitated.

"Actually Mama, she is coming here tomorrow."

"Oh, my dear, what a terrible encroaching female! Couldn't you have put her off?"

"I am afraid not. I invited her."

"But you said you do not like her."

"I didn't precisely say that."

"*Bossy*, you said."

"And so she is."

"Then she must have forced you to invite her."

"Not exactly. It was my own idea, and I am sending a carriage to collect her," John replied, growing more awkward by the moment as he saw his mother staring at him as if he had gone out of his mind.

There was a silence, during which a variety of thoughts passed across Lady Evelyn's face. But she was far too clever to let her son suspect which one had made the most lasting impression on her.

"Very well, my dear," she said at last. "I suppose you know your own business best."

John shook his head.

"Oh, no. I am beginning to think I am the very last person who knows my business best," he said, beginning to feel light-headed. "Perhaps I should ask Miss Wilton. She knows all about it, far better than I do."

He did not wait long enough for his astonished mother to ask any more questions, but kissed her and hurried away.

When he reached his bedroom he was horrified at how dilapidated it was. The four-poster bed had been magnificent when it was first built, with splendid gold ornamentation and crimson brocade hangings that were echoed in the curtains.

Now the hangings were threadbare and in some places actually in tatters.

They were dusty too, John thought, brushing them down and then wishing he had not, as he began to cough.

It was a large room with two huge windows and a vast fireplace that looked impressive, but which, John knew, was incredibly draughty.

The paper on the walls was peeling. The woodwork needed repainting and the chairs, of which there were four, were all damaged in some way or another. The carpet was worn and torn in various places.

He tried the mattress gingerly and it felt as though it was stuffed with turnips.

'But then, it always did,' he mused. 'The curtains were always shabby, but now they are falling to pieces.'

He tried not to look at the ceiling, which he knew was covered with frescoes of mythical deities and their attendants. Cherubs chased each other across impossibly blue skies as nymphs glanced flirtatiously at strapping young Gods. The vulgarity of the whole decor had always made John shudder.

At last he gave in and glanced up. Then he shuddered again.

The best that could be said was that the damage hid the worst of the cherubs. A fungus like growth was creeping across the ceiling, obscuring the pictures as it went.

'And this is just one room,' he thought.

There was a knock on the door. Opening it, he was surprised to find two elderly women, each bearing trays. As he stood back they made a stately procession into the apartment and set their trays down on two low tables. They contained tea and sandwiches and John had to admit that it all looked very appetising.

"Good evening, Your Grace," said the first woman.

"Good evening, Your Grace," said the second.

Blinking, John realised that they were as alike as two peas in a pod. Not only did they have the same face, but they were dressed identically in blue dresses that looked as though they had once been expensive, but were now old and shabby.

"Good evening," he said, somewhat at a loss. "I am the new Duke."

"Yes, Your Grace, we know that."

"I am very glad to meet you. Did you work for my uncle for very long?"

"We didn't work for him," said one. "We were his friends."

"I beg your pardon?"

40

"He took us in," said the other. "We were homeless, so he said we should come and live with him."

John began to understand. These were lost sheep.

"I am Imelda."

"And I am Sonia."

"How do you do – er – ladies."

He was unsure how to address them but their voices were cultured, making a strange contrast to their appearance. So it seemed safer to assume that they were ladies.

"Jeremiah says that he hopes you enjoy the food, Your Grace. He has done his best in the circumstances, but not knowing that Your Grace was arriving tonight – "

"Jeremiah?" John interrupted desperately. "Wasn't my uncle's cook called Howard?"

"Mr. Howard departed," declared Imelda. Or it might have been Sonia.

"Why?"

"His pay was in arrears, Your Grace," said Sonia. Or it might have been Imelda.

"What about Jeremiah?"

"Jeremiah does not need to be paid," said one of them.

So Jeremiah too was a lost sheep, he deduced.

"Well – thank you!"

"We hope you will be very happy here, Your Grace."

"There's no need to say 'Your Grace' every time," he said. "Just 'sir' will do."

"Oh, no, Your Grace. That would *not* be proper. You are the Duke."

"So everyone keeps reminding me. Yesterday I was simply John Chester. Now I am the ninth Duke of Chesterton."

"Tenth," piped up one of the twins.

"What?"

"The late Duke was the ninth," said the other twin. "Your Grace is the tenth."

"Are you sure?"

"Quite sure, Your Grace."

He did not try to argue. Clearly everyone for miles around knew his position and what was due to him far better than he did. Gina had been only the start.

"I am sure you are right. In future, please just call me sir."

"Yes, Your Grace."

They gave him brief nods and, turning, made another procession out of the room.

John tore his hair, wondering if he was in a madhouse, and if so, was it really *his* madhouse?

The food, at least, was excellent, he thought, devouring it hungrily. And the tea was just as he liked it.

But that was only one small light in the darkness. The mood that Gina had talked him into was fading. Her idea of restoring the castle was just a fairy tale.

'An impractical dream,' he thought. 'And somehow she made me believe it.'

Then he wondered if he was being feeble and knew that Gina would certainly think so. He remembered the excitement in her voice as she told him her ideas and the light that had shone from her eyes.

'I cannot let her down,' he told himself.

He wondered why it should be so important to someone he had only just met.

'Why should it matter so much to her?' he asked himself.

Somehow he was afraid of the answer to that question.

The following morning he was up and dressed long before the rest of his family appeared.

He walked from his bedroom (he could not bring himself to call it the Royal Apartment) into the front of the castle where the worst damage had been to the roof and the two wings.

One wing seemed to have almost collapsed completely. Everywhere he looked, he found more to depress him.

'Whatever can I do?' John asked himself.

As if in answer, he heard a crash in the distance.

'It's a sign,' he told himself. 'Some higher power is telling me that there is nothing to be done. I won't even have to explain to Gina. She will see for herself how hopeless it is.'

He ran downstairs and outside to get a better look. He found an elderly man staring up into the sky. At his feet was a lump of stone, which must have just missed him.

"Are you all right?" John asked him anxiously.

"Oh, yes, perfectly, my dear fellow," said the old man. "Just a bit of sky came down."

"It seems to be a bit of wall."

The man looked at him vaguely.

"Really? Oh, dear no, I don't think so. The walls are perfectly strong and sturdy, you know. Never saw better. But sometimes the sky comes down."

He indicated the stone at his feet.

John regarded him warily. He was beginning to understand that this man had his own way of seeing things.

"It's the wrong colour for sky," he pointed out. "It's grey and surely sky is blue?"

"Oh, but it was blue when it began its journey," his companion assured him earnestly. "But travelling all that distance – it undergoes a metamorphosis."

"I see. Yes, you may be right. By the way, how do you do? I am John Chester."

"The new Duke. Yes, I know. I am Pharaoh."

"Pharaoh? You mean, a King?"

"My dear fellow, you are too kind. I don't insist on the formalities. Pharaoh will do."

"Then you had better call me John," he said, thankful that he had finally found someone to sympathise with his desire for informality.

But he was disappointed again.

"Call you John?" echoed Pharaoh, aghast. "Oh, no, I couldn't do that, Your Grace. The proprieties must be observed."

"But you – "

"Oh, I rise above it all. I think that's why the sky keeps trying to descend on me. It makes sense, you know."

"Yes," John murmured, glassy eyed. "I am beginning to think it does."

"It's almost time for breakfast, I think. Shall we go in?" Pharaoh asked graciously.

Together they made their way to the breakfast room, where Lady Evelyn was just entering. This was John's first encounter with the strange arrangements that now prevailed at the castle. The food was cooked by Jeremiah and served by Sonia and Imelda. After which they all met at the table and sat down together.

He began to see that there were complications. Were the lost sheep servants who had to be treated as friends or friends doing the work of servants?

While he was still trying to work it out he found himself sitting down next to Pharaoh and accepting a plate of bacon and eggs.

"My son is bringing a visitor to see us this morning," Lady Evelyn announced. "Miss Gina Wilton. We must all make her very welcome."

Everybody muttered assent and kindly words with as much graciousness as courtiers.

As soon as he decently could, John left the breakfast table. He was anxious to see more of the house before Gina arrived.

What he discovered depressed him even more.

Everywhere he saw decay, neglect and the desperate need of money. He knew that if he had any sense he would send a message to Gina telling her not to come here.

But that would be unkind, he reasoned. Besides, it was better for her to see why her idea would not work. Otherwise, she would give him no peace about it.

He went to the stables and found a lad.

"I want someone to take the carriage to this address," he said, producing the piece of paper with Gina's address. "Who is the coachman here now?"

"Pharaoh does that, Your Grace."

"Of course he does," John muttered. "Why didn't I think of that before?"

He spent the next hour on hot coals, rehearsing the speech in which he would tell Gina to forget all about their glorious, impossible plans.

But when she arrived, looking pretty and excited, he knew he was not brave enough to disappoint her.

From a distance she waved at him and he waved back, keeping his eyes fixed on the approaching carriage.

It was becoming impossible to do anything except

what this forceful girl wanted, and that was more alarming than anything else that had happened to him.

As she ran towards him he could only hold out his hands and say,

"It is so good to see you. I hope I didn't send the carriage too early, but I was eager to resume our talk."

'And eager to see you,' he thought.

"Come to meet my mother," he proposed. "And we will look around afterwards."

He noticed that her clothes, although good, were rather severe. Her coat was plain and on her head she wore a straw boater. Beneath her coat she had on a skirt and a garment that might have been a blouse, but which looked more like a man's shirt with a tie.

He knew some women dressed in this mannish fashion and had always thought it highly unsuitable. But on her it was delightful.

As he led her across the hall, he realised that she was looking around her with increasing dismay.

"I warned you," he murmured.

"It is very bad," she agreed. "But are we faint hearted?"

"Well, yes, I think we might be," he admitted.

"Nonsense! We are *not* faint-hearted! We are determined! We are resolute! We do not admit the possibility of defeat."

"I don't think I could go as far as that."

"Never mind. You will."

After a few more steps she said,

"Your Grace – "

"John," he said desperately. "If one more person calls me 'Your Grace', I'll jump out of a high window."

"John, who are those people staring at me?"

"Where?"

He followed her gaze up the stairs and was just in time to see several faces vanish.

"Those are my uncle's friends," he said, grinning. There are the twins, Imelda and Sonia, Jeremiah who cooks like an angel and Pharaoh who tries to keep the sky in place."

"Who – ?"

"I will explain later," he mumbled hastily. "We have nearly reached Mama's room. Please tell her nothing of what we discussed yesterday, because I haven't mentioned it to her yet."

"Oh, good!" she said with an enthusiasm that filled him with alarm. "Because since yesterday I have thought of several ways to improve my plan."

Then, having done what she could to set his mind at rest, she slipped her hand in his arm and accompanied him into Lady Evelyn's room.

CHAPTER FOUR

John saw that his mother was dressed in a gown that he had seen two years earlier, but which she wore with such style that she looked most elegant. Nobody would gave guessed that she had to be thrifty, he thought with admiration.

She greeted Gina charmingly and looked her over without being too obvious about it.

"My dear girl," she said. "John has told me all about you."

John wished he could hide.

"Indeed, ma'am, I hope he has not," Gina answered earnestly.

"Really? Why?"

"Well, would you like to think that any gentleman knew all about you?" Gina asked with a twinkle.

Lady Evelyn made a sudden, alert movement.

"You are quite right," she said. "It would be intolerable. My own dear husband never knew all about me until the day he died, I am happy to say."

One of the twins glided into the room with a tea tray, set it down and began to pour.

"John says you are a school marm," declared Lady Evelyn.

"No, Mama, I didn't exactly – "

"Then he really doesn't know all about me," Gina said with a chuckle. "I only told him that I was interested in becoming a teacher because I have nothing to do. I did not actually say that I was one."

"I see. He must have misunderstood, probably through fear and dread."

"Fear and dread?" Gina enquired.

"My son, Miss Wilton, is the old-fashioned kind of man who regards a well educated woman with horror."

John covered his eyes.

"Are you well educated?" Lady Evelyn asked.

"I am afraid I am, your Ladyship," Gina said apologetically. "My mother was a vicar's daughter and her Papa taught her Greek and Latin, as well as mathematics, logic, French, Italian and literature, all of which she passed on to me.

"I did go to school for a short time, but Mama was not satisfied with the education they provided. It was footling stuff, history in pictures and so forth. We were taught to name flowers and write sickly verse, but not to analyse a sentence.

"So Mama took me away. At the end of his life Grandpapa came to live with us and after that I learned from him."

"You have studied Greek and Latin?" Lady Evelyn asked in an awed whisper.

"And philosophy, history and science," Gina finished with a triumphant air of tidying up ends.

"But my dear girl, have you never learned the art of hiding all this academic achievement, for fear of frightening suitors away?"

"I have no intention of hiding it," Gina proclaimed

49

proudly. "If a man is so feeble that my education scares him, then he is not the man for me. I would abominate such a man. I would crush him beneath my heel and tell him to be gone, lest I smite him!"

"Well done, Miss Wilton," exclaimed Lady Evelyn at once. "I admire your spirit. Though I must warn you that most men are such poor-spirited creatures that if you crush all the feeble ones, there will be none left."

"But would we be any worse off without them, ma'am?" Gina asked mischievously.

"Indeed we would not," said Lady Evelyn.

"Shall I go away?" John asked politely. "It is quite clear that my presence is not required."

His mother regarded him over the rim of her spectacles.

"John dear, are you still here? To be honest, I thought you had already gone away."

"I am willing to depart if my presence annoys you, Mama."

"Oh, no, my dear. I am sure we can find a use for you."

"I am prepared to conduct Miss Wilton around the castle whenever she wishes," he said.

He was afraid that his mother had taken against Gina, and her behaviour was meant as an unmistakable warning that such a clever female would not suit him.

This struck him as unreasonable. It was not Gina's fault that she was clever. Unscrupulous persons had indoctrinated her while she was too young to protest. It was unjust to hold it against her and he would inform his mother so at the first available opportunity.

But it seemed that the opportunity would not be quick in coming. Gina declared that she would much rather stay and talk to Lady Evelyn than to see around the castle just now, so John wandered away feeling unwanted.

His footsteps took him into the grounds and he realised with a certain melancholy that the beautiful weather was showing the castle at its best. Just standing here, you could hardly tell how shabby it was inside.

He found Pharaoh sitting under a tree with a sketchbook, making a charcoal sketch of the castle.

"But that's excellent!"

"I have a certain facility," the old man agreed. "I dabble. I pass the time." He sighed as though labouring under some great tragedy.

John moved on, strolling in the direction of the great gate that formed the entrance. And there he stopped, gaping at something he saw.

A carriage was rumbling through the gate. It was occupied by a young and very pretty girl who stood up and waved as soon as she saw him.

Behind her was a fourgon piled high with baggage, most of which, he saw with a groan, looked brand new.

"*Johnnneeee!*" called the girl, still waving madly.

John ground his teeth. He hated to be called Johnny.

As the carriage came to a halt she jumped down and came flying towards him, to hurl her arms about his neck.

"Johnny! Johnny. My darling brother!" she squealed.

"Hallo, Drusilla," he said, trying not to stagger under the impact. "My, how you have changed. I wouldn't have recognised you."

"I am different, aren't I?" she squawked. "Much, much more grown up."

She jumped back and twirled round again and again, so that her new clothes were displayed to best advantage.

John tried not to think about what they must have cost.

No doubt the bills would reach him soon.

And to them would be added the bills for this carriage, and the fourgon and the men who were unloading the mountain of bags and looking at him expectantly.

"Bring them inside," he said curtly and walked into the castle, followed by a small procession.

"You had better take them right up to my room," Drusilla ordered airily.

John was about to protest when he realised that the shortage of servants in the castle made this an impractical idea. But he groaned at the thought of the extra tip this would involve.

"I am afraid that there is no room prepared for you," he said, leading the way upstairs.

In fact, since Drusilla had never lived in the castle there was no room set aside as hers. Finding one would involve an extensive search to find something that was not in too bad a state.

He stopped hastily on the landing.

"You can leave the bags here," he said, reaching into his pocket for a coin.

But to his surprise the men waved his money away.

"Thank you, sir, but we've already been paid. Good day to you, sir."

Dumbfounded, John watched as they walked downstairs and out through the front door.

"Are you in the Royal Apartment now that you're the Duke?" Drusilla wanted to know.

"Yes," he groaned.

"Come on, show me."

She grabbed his hand and began to drag him toward the Royal Apartment. As he had expected she was not impressed.

"You need to have it redecorated," she said decisively.

"Never mind that. What are you doing home, Drusilla? You should be at Finishing School. Heaven knows it costs me enough, so you should at least stay until the end of term."

"Pooh, what does it matter what things cost?" she asked blithely. "I came home because Finishing School had nothing more to teach me."

"I think they still have a great deal to teach you, including manners and decorum."

"Silly! That's not what Finishing School is for."

"Really?"

"Yes, really. It's for teaching you how to snare a rich husband."

"They didn't knock the vulgarity out of you, I see."

"Well, it's true. They talk about giving you 'finish' and 'polish' as though you were a piece of furniture. They brag about the 'accomplishments' they teach you, like French and music, and dancing. But the whole point is to find a rich husband and everyone knows it, although nobody says it."

John wished he could think of a reply, but he had a horrible feeling that it was true.

"The real accomplishment," Drusilla rattled on, "is knowing how to spend your husband's money with taste and elegance."

"Taste and elegance?" he echoed with brotherly scepticism. "You?"

"I have extremely sophisticated tastes in jewellery and clothes," she assured him. "I like only the best."

"And if that was enough to find you a rich husband all my cares would be over," John declared. "Unfortunately men with money can take their pick and the ability to be extravagant is not enough to attract them."

Drusilla giggled.

"That is what *you* think, brother dear."

"What are you talking about?"

"I told you I didn't need Finishing School any more, because it was just to help me bag a rich husband. Well, I have got one for myself. So I came home."

"You what?" he gasped.

"I've got a rich husband. So I'll soon be off your hands. Won't that be a relief to you?"

John's head was spinning.

"Drusilla," he managed to say at last, "you are seventeen years old."

"I know that."

"But what you don't seem to know is the way to behave. You don't want the world to call you an incorrigible flirt, do you?"

"It doesn't matter once I am married. They can say what they like."

"I see. And what about your husband's feelings?"

"Oh, I'll keep him sweet. He is madly in love with me, so that's all right."

"And what about you? Are you in love with him?"

"Oh, Johnny, darling! He's got fifty thousand pounds a year. Of course I am in love with him."

John gulped. Fifty thousand pounds a year! Was there so much money in the world?

Then his brotherly protectiveness asserted itself.

"Who is this man, Dru?"

She winced.

"Please, Johnny! Not 'Dru'. It's so common."

"I will call you Drusilla if you will stop calling me Johnny. You know I hate it."

"All right, it's a bargain. Dear, dear Johnny!"

"Drusilla, you must tell me something about this man. I need to know more than his bank balance."

"You need to know? I am the one who will be marrying him."

"If I give my consent. I am, after all, the *Head of the Family*."

The effect of this pronouncement was disconcerting. His sister threw back her head and positively shrieked with laughter.

"Oh, Johnny, you are so funny!"

"I don't mean to be."

"But it is funny! You, *Head of the Family*! It's a positive scream."

"Well, if you want my consent to this marriage, let me advise you not to scream too loudly," he asserted, feeling distinctly huffy. Surely a Duke was entitled to some respect from his younger sister?

"Tell me who he is," he insisted. "Do I know him?"

"I shouldn't think so. He's a grocer."

"A grocer? Have you taken leave of your senses?"

"But a grocer with fifty thousand a year."

"How can he have? My poor girl, he has been spinning yarns to turn your head – "

"Oh, Johnny dear, don't be so silly. He doesn't go around on a bicycle, delivering fruit. He has other people to do that for him. He owns hundreds of grocer's shops."

"How old is he?"

"About forty-five, fifty, I'm not sure."

"A middle-aged tradesman!"

"A very rich tradesman," she corrected him.

"I don't care how rich he is, you cannot marry him."

"You know nothing about him," she cried.

"On the contrary, I think I know exactly what he is like. He has probably got a red face, a pot belly and huge side whiskers. If I am so misguided as to meet him he'll clap me on the back and call me *Squire*!"

"Does that really matter?"

It did matter for more reasons than John could have explained. With Drusilla he did not even try. Another thought had occurred to him.

"I know what it is," he said. "You are sacrificing yourself for the family."

"What?"

"Knowing the dire straits I find myself in you have found a rich man to help the situation, but my dear sister, your duty to your family doesn't extend to – "

At this point he gave up. Drusilla was looking at him blankly and it was clear she had not understood a word he said. The word 'duty' was especially confusing to this spoilt child.

"You are not marrying a grocer just because he has money," he said flatly.

"Then find me someone else with money," she snapped, the sunshine disappearing from her face. "Do you think I want to be trapped in this old barn all my life just because you can't give me a dowry?"

She burst into violent tears.

At once John put his arms about her.

"Don't cry. I'll find a way to make it all right."

If only he knew how, he thought.

"You are home now," he said, "so let's just enjoy being reunited. There's someone I want you to meet, but first let's go and find Mama. She will be so happy to see you."

Drusilla sniffed and wiped her eyes.

"All right, but I haven't changed my mind. I am going to marry Arthur."

"Arthur?"

"Arthur Scuggins."

He gave an inward groan. He might have known that the grocer would have a name like Arthur Scuggins.

"You simply cannot go through life with a name like Scuggins," he said. "Think of it, Dru. You couldn't – "

She stamped her foot.

"Don't call me that. I will do what I like. I won't be poor, I won't!"

"Well, I certainly agree that you need a husband with a large income," he sighed. "It took my breath away to see the extravagant way you travelled home. That carriage alone must have cost a fortune to hire. However did you pay for it?"

"I didn't. It's Arthur's."

"What?"

"And the fourgon. And the men."

"You travelled home at this man's expense? Have you no sense of propriety?"

"No, I don't think I have. What does it matter since I am going to marry him?"

John opened his mouth and then closed it again. There was little he could say or do about this situation without compromising his sister.

One issue was clear.

Like it or not, he would have to meet this man and pay him. Next he would have to ask a lot of questions and be prepared for answers that he did not like.

"Let's go down and find Mama," he insisted.

On the landing they discovered that some of Drusilla's

bags had been moved, and one of the twins was supervising the removal of the rest by a middle aged man.

"Thank you, er – "

"Imelda," she said, taking pity on him. "I am taking them to the blue room, Your Grace. It is being made ready now."

"Thank you," he said with fervour, grateful for someone who understood his problems.

Downstairs he took Drusilla to find their mother, who was still deep in conversation with Gina. As soon as they entered, Lady Evelyn rose to her feet and held out her arms to her daughter in welcome.

While they were hugging each other and exclaiming, John took the chance to draw Gina aside.

"They will want to be alone for a while," he muttered. "I am sorry to have left you alone with my mother. Did she make life very difficult for you?"

"No, she was very nice. Why should you think she was unkind?"

"I didn't exactly mean unkind," he said hastily. "It's just that sometimes Mama gets an idea into her head and she forgets everything else."

Gina's baffled look warned him to stop there. He could hardly tell her that his mother was afraid that he meant to marry her and had been trying to warn him off. Nor could he say that nothing was further from his thoughts than marrying a bluestocking, lovely though she was.

"Have you thought up any more good ideas?" he asked to change the subject.

"Oh, yes!" She turned suddenly and clasped his hands. "I have good news, John, very good news."

"Tell me quickly."

"My father and two friends, who came to dinner with

him last night, were very enthusiastic at our idea. When I went to bed all three of them were working out how much they could spend on the castle."

"Already? Is it possible?"

"All we have to do now is find lots of other people."

"That's all we have to do?"

"Yes, but that's simple if we do what we discussed in the carriage yesterday – call people here to the castle to let them see the problem for themselves. It is not just a question of only the rich, but everyone who lives in the County. It matters to all of them. And when it has been restored people will come and see it and they will spend money and the whole area will prosper."

Again her excitement made John wonder if he was dreaming.

'How can it mean so much to her?' he wondered. 'She must have countless men pursuing her, wanting to dance with her, to talk to her and to kiss her. And all she cares about is a ruin.'

She had never even been here before, yet she spoke as though it was her personal responsibility to protect the castle. And if she could persuade others to feel the same, they would follow her lead.

The shops would benefit, so would the Churches and hotels. The roads would have to be enlarged and made easier to travel on, so that every year there would be more and more visitors to the castle.

And all because Miss Gina Wilton possessed the soul of a pioneer, he thought, with a rising excitement that matched hers.

"I don't know who to invite to this meeting. But I feel sure that you do."

"Well, I have a list that Papa made up for me," she said, producing a piece of paper. "He says these are the oldest families in the County. He is also making another list of those who arrived so recently that they are not on this list."

John took the paper from her and saw it was longer than he expected. As he read the names and addresses, he felt that Gina's father knew a great deal more about the County than he knew himself.

He was surprised at the importance of some of the names. There were families he had heard of years ago, but had not been in touch with them for so long that he had forgotten their very existence.

"Do I have to speak to all these people?" he asked.

"Of course. They will want to hear everything from your own lips," Gina replied. "I think we should ask them not for this Saturday but the following one."

"You have relieved my mind. I had visions of you summoning them for tomorrow. You are the last person I expected to counsel delay."

"We must give people time to accept and it would be a great mistake, Papa thinks, for you to risk this meeting going badly because it was rushed. And of course, this will not be the only list."

"Good Heavens! Is somebody going to make another one?"

"Why you are, of course. There is bound to be some record of the late Duke's friends and associates. Do you know where your uncle wrote his letters?"

"In the library, I suppose. That would be the place to start."

As they headed for the library John did not speak, but he knew that Gina was looking at the walls where the paper was peeling.

When they reached the library he thought it was a disgrace. The windows were cracked. The floor was dirty

60

and the desk should have been thrown away before it collapsed completely.

"What a nightmare!" John exclaimed. "I wouldn't know where to begin looking."

Even as he spoke there was the sound of footsteps and a tall thin man came into the room. He was about forty and good looking in a quiet way. He gave John a small, elegant bow.

"Good morning, Your Grace. Allow me to introduce myself. I was your late uncle's secretary and now I am yours. I am Ambrose Faber."

John shook his hand.

"Why, now I remember you," he said pleasantly. "When I was a child I used to play here at the castle and sometimes you were visiting here."

"I was hardly visiting," Ambrose answered with a smile. "Your uncle allowed me to run errands for him in return for my board and lodging. Last year I returned and did my best to be useful to him. Now I hope I can be useful to you."

"And so you can be," John replied. "I am sure you know what a bad way everything is in."

Faber sighed and nodded.

"Miss Wilton here has an idea that may save us. We are planning a reception to be given here and everyone on this list is to be invited. There will be more names to follow and as the reception is to be on Saturday week, I am afraid that doesn't give you much time."

To his surprise Ambrose smiled and said,

"You were the same as a child, Your Grace. Here today and gone tomorrow, making everyone run to get things done."

"But this time it isn't I who is ordering the running," John responded with a significant glance at Gina who was watching them both with an innocent look. Just as though she had not been responsible for the whole thing, he thought indignantly.

"I think," he said, "that Miss Wilton and I should tell you what we are planning. Together," he added firmly.

So they told him with both of them more or less talking at once.

"Do you really intend having all these people in the castle?" Ambrose managed to say when he could get a word in edgeways.

"These and a great many more," John replied. "In fact, we are asking everyone in the County to come to what will be the most important gathering ever held in the castle."

"But, to what end?" Ambrose asked, bewildered.

Gina then told him the whole plan in detail.

At first he could only gasp.

When she had finally stopped speaking, he said,

"It's incredible, but it might work."

"Of course it will work," Gina burst out. "We will have the most famous and the most beautiful castle in the whole of England."

"Then I had better go and start work," he said, and departed.

When they were alone John looked at Gina who was bubbling over with excitement. She looked prettier than ever and he had to remind himself that she was a dreaded bluestocking, or she might have enchanted him.

"Why don't I show you the castle now?" he suggested.

"Oh, yes, please. I have dreamed of it all my life and now that I am here I want to make the most of it."

With a flourish he offered her his arm.

"In that case, madam, allow me to escort you. Dilapidated though it is, my home is at your service."

CHAPTER FIVE

Chesterton Castle was one of the oldest in the country.

"That's why it's so special," Gina enthused as they went to look at the moat. "A real Norman castle, one of the first built by William the Conqueror on lands given by him to Baron Guy le Chester."

She sounded as though she was reciting a lesson learned by heart.

"Was it?" John asked.

"Don't pretend that you don't know," she chided him, laughing. "This is your heritage, your glory. When I think how you must swell with pride to think that you are descended from Baron Guy le Chester, Swithin Chester who fought with the Black Prince, Algernon Chester who was one of Queen Elizabeth's courtiers – "

"I hate to disappoint you," he interrupted her hastily, "but I do not swell with pride. When I was a boy I thought it was an intolerable bore having to learn all those names."

"Really?" she sounded shocked.

"Really. I know what a poor creature you must think me now, but it cannot be helped."

He sighed and tried to look convincingly dejected by his own failure.

"Oh, well," she said at last. "It cannot be helped. One must allow something for the vagaries of youth."

"I was a horrible child," he said, throwing another ember on the fire.

"I am sure you were, but one cannot expect children to appreciate their history. One must take a larger view."

"Miss Wilton," he said with feeling, "if you don't stop being so appallingly reasonable and understanding, I shall do something desperate."

She giggled and it had a strange effect on him, as though a shiver of delight had gone right through him. The temptation to tease her was suddenly irresistible.

"Besides, I did not grow up in the castle. My family lived in a house on the estate. Everyone assumed that my uncle would marry and his son would inherit. So I wasn't, as you seem to assume, reared in the knowledge of my destiny."

"Oh, dear," she sighed.

"I was just an ordinary boy. I climbed trees and played truant."

"But weren't you entranced by the romance of a castle that has stood all these centuries?"

"No," he said firmly. "Now, let us start our exploration. This was the original keep."

As he spoke he led her towards the great round tower.

It was the highest part of the castle, having been constructed on top of a small hill so that it dominated not only the rest of the building but the whole countryside. It was built of white stone, with narrow slit windows.

"Did archers stand behind those windows to fire arrows at invaders?" Gina asked eagerly.

"Certainly they did."

She gave a sigh of relief.

"That's all right then," she said happily.

"What a very bloodthirsty young woman you are, to be sure!"

"Not at all. But wars are part of history and a true student must look at the entire picture. I hold it a poor thing for any female to befuddle her mind with pretty pictures of the past, when the truth is really far more exciting, even if more gruesome."

"Indeed!" said John, shocked by this unfeminine toughness of mind. "Well, you must remind me to show you the dungeons, complete with instruments of torture. You will have a wonderful time."

"Oh, yes, please!"

John had always found the keep rather gloomy and dank, but Gina went round it with eyes wide and entranced. Everything was wonderful to her.

"I used to dream of this when I was a child," she said eagerly. "From my bedroom window I could see this very tower silhouetted against the sky and I would think of all the thrilling events that unfolded here."

"They weren't fighting invaders all the time," John objected. "This was a living area. These were the servants' quarters at the bottom and then we climb up to where the family lived."

"It isn't stone inside," she said, sounding disappointed.

"No, the inside is made of timber and it's not in very good repair, so be careful how you go."

The upper stories were shabby with tapestries and hangings in rags. In one great bedroom a four-poster bed stood with one of its posts missing and a corner hanging drunkenly down.

But nothing could dampen Gina's spirits. She wandered blissfully from room to room, sometimes closing her eyes and just standing still, clearly full of visions. John watched her, smiling kindly.

"Is it as good as you had hoped?" he enquired.

"Oh, it's wonderful. Just think how people must have felt, living here."

"Chilly, I should think. This place would have been incredibly draughty even when the hangings weren't falling to pieces."

She did not seem to hear. She had wandered over to one of the narrow windows and was looking out over the countryside.

John came to stand beside her and for the first time he realised just how far it was possible to see from this high place.

For miles and miles the view stretched. And on the other side of the keep the view would stretch as far. The men and women who had lived here had reason to feel that they were the rulers of all they surveyed.

And the people, in turn, had been able to see this tower from a great distance. In fact, they could not escape it. John began to understand what Gina was talking about when she said that everyone had a stake in the castle and a kind of excitement stirred in him.

"Are we right at the top?" she asked.

"Just one more floor."

They left the great room and walked to the wooden staircase that led to the top. Gina immediately began to climb it, eager to see more.

Suddenly there was an ominous creaking noise and the step beneath her foot gave way, then the one beneath that.

The next moment she was falling.

Quick as lightning, John held up his arms and caught her before she landed, clasping her tightly.

"Oh, thank you," she gasped.

He was holding her high against his chest, one arm under her knees, one supporting her back. Somehow her arms were about his neck and she was looking up into his face.

He looked down at her and her face seemed to swim before him. In the gloom her eyes looked enormous, gazing up at him.

He could feel her warm breath fluttering against his mouth.

He was aware that he ought to set her down, as propriety demanded, but he could not move. And he knew in his heart that he did not want to move. He wanted to stay here like this, holding her warm body against his own, until he lowered his mouth to hers and then –

He drew a deep, shuddering breath.

"Are you all right?" he asked hoarsely.

"What?" she whispered.

"Are you hurt?"

"No," she replied. "You caught me in time."

"I am – glad."

He had the alarming feeling that he was not making sense. His head was still spinning.

"John – " she said raggedly, "I think you should put me down."

"Yes – yes, of course."

Slowly he lowered her until her feet touched the ground and felt her hands tighten against his shoulders to steady herself. Even so, she staggered a little when he released her.

"Are you quite sure you weren't hurt?" he asked in a low voice.

"No – no – I am just – a little giddy. It scared me, that's all."

"Perhaps we should go back," he said. "I will show you the rest later."

He preceded her down the stairs to the bottom of the tower, so that he would be there if she fell again, but nothing happened.

As they walked away from the keep and back to the main part of the castle, where the family now lived, John was talking to himself very severely.

He did not know what had possessed him during those few blinding moments when he had held Gina in his arms, but he knew that it had been very dangerous.

He liked her well enough, but she was the last person in the world he would want to marry. She was bossy, interfering, intellectual, all the things a woman definitely should *not* be.

Yet he had been on the verge of kissing her, dazzled by a mysterious aura that had come from her while their bodies were so close.

That must never happen again, he told himself. He could not send her away, since he planned to use her ideas, but he would keep her at a proper distance.

He stole a sideways glance at Gina to see if she reflected any of his own consciousness of what had happened. But she was not looking at him and except for a certain pallor, she seemed unaffected.

"You will meet my sister, Drusilla," he said as they entered the house. "She arrived home from Finishing School half an hour ago with windmills in her head."

"What kind of windmills."

"She is convinced that she has snared a wealthy husband."

"But that's wonderful," Gina breathed. "Why he could help – "

"Miss Wilton," he said wrathfully, "could you please forget the castle for just one moment? There are other things in the world that are of interest."

"Surely not, Your Grace."

He ground his teeth.

"I assure you, Drusilla has no thought of helping the family. She simply wishes to live an extravagant life and she's prepared to marry a tra – a fat, elderly grocer to do it."

Gina looked at him mischievously.

"You were about to say 'tradesman', weren't you?"

"I forget what I was about to say."

"Yes, you were. Then you remembered that my father is a builder – a tradesman."

"Your father has produced an estimable daughter and I have the highest regard for him," John said, wishing the earth would open and swallow him up. "Besides which, your grandfather is a vicar."

"Does that make a difference?" she asked innocently.

It did, of course, make a difference, since a vicar was a gentleman and a tradesman was not. But John did not feel equal to saying any of this, especially with her challenging eyes on him.

"You know perfectly well what I mean."

"Of course I do and it's shocking of me to make fun of you."

"Yes, it is," he said with feeling.

"Then I won't do so any more. Besides, we have more important things to consider. This fat, elderly grocer – "

"Arthur Scuggins," he informed her.

"That is his name?" she asked faintly.

"Indeed it is!"

"Oh, well, it cannot be helped. Is Arthur Scuggins a *wealthy* fat, elderly grocer?"

"Drusilla seems to think that he is."

"In that case, Your Grace – "

"What do you mean 'Your Grace'? You were going to call me John."

"And you were going to call me Gina, but I have mysteriously become Miss Wilton again."

"Yes – well – "

He floundered to a standstill, since it was not possible to tell her that this was part of his plan to set her at a safe distance.

They entered the drawing room to find tea and cakes being served by one of the twins, who immediately hurried away to fetch more.

Drusilla rose from where she had been sitting enjoying a cosy chat with her mother and John introduced the two girls.

He could not help comparing them. Drusilla, niece of one Duke, sister of another, looked overdressed and fussy. Gina, daughter of a builder, looked quietly elegant and her manner was restrained. Of the two, it was she who appeared to be the lady. Drusilla, he reckoned, was bidding fair to become a hoyden.

More tea and cakes appeared and John discovered that they were the best cakes he had ever tasted. The tea too was excellent and so had the breakfast been, he recalled. Clearly Jeremiah, the lost sheep who had taken over the kitchen, was an expert, which was something to be thankful for.

Gina described her morning looking round the keep and Lady Evelyn gave a shudder.

"Dreadful mouldy place," she exclaimed. "In fact, so is the whole castle. I shall be glad to move back to our own home."

"Oh, Mama," Drusilla said with a little shriek. "We cannot live in that pokey little place. Not now we are grand. A Duke's family should live in a castle."

"Except that the castle is impossible to live in," said John, resisting the temptation to tear his hair.

"But we are going to make it right," Gina objected.

"How?" Drusilla wanted to know.

Seeing John look nonplussed, Gina whispered,

"Shouldn't I have said anything?"

"No, it is time we told Mama what we are going to do," John said.

Briefly he outlined Gina's plan to his astonished mother.

"But that's wonderful!" Drusilla exclaimed. "Then everything will be all right and we'll be as grand as we ought to be."

"That isn't why I am doing it," John answered. "It is to preserve our heritage for the sake of everyone in the area."

"Oh, who cares about them? It will be glorious for us," said Drusilla.

"No," Lady Evelyn said decisively. "Your brother is right. We are not doing this for ourselves, but for history. Gina, my dear, it is an excellent idea. I shall help you as much as I can and I expect to be involved in everything."

"Of course, ma'am," said Gina, jumping to her feet in her excitement.

Lady Evelyn also rose and took her hands.

"And you must come and stay here, my dear."

"Mama!" John exclaimed frantically.

"But your Ladyship, I cannot – "

"Of course you can. If you are going to arrange all this you need to be in the centre of it. You cannot keep coming and going every day. You must live here as part of the family. Oh, do say yes, do!"

"Yes!" exclaimed Gina. "Oh, yes, *please*."

Drusilla too bounded to her feet, squealing with excitement and joined the other two, dancing round and round, hand in hand, while John regarded the three of them, aghast at the calamity that had befallen him.

For the sake of his sanity he had planned to keep her at a safe distance. Now she was to live under his roof.

Gina spent the rest of the day working with Ambrose on lists, while John took himself off to visit other parts of his estate. He was afraid he might not be able to hide his dismay that she would continue to be there.

It was arranged that she would return to her home that evening to collect her luggage and come back to the castle next morning. John saw her into the carriage, thanked her for her work and stood watching as she departed, wondering at himself for the way he felt.

Gina had a strange magic and that was dangerous. He would have avoided her if he could, but now that was impossible.

*

An hour later the carriage pulled up outside Gina's home, a large stone mansion set in extensive grounds. As she descended, a powdered footman pulled open the front door.

"Good evening, miss."

"Good evening, Cadmon. Are my parents in?"

"In the library, miss."

As she headed for the library another powdered footman opened the door for her.

Her Mama was standing on the hearthrug, twisting and turning before her father, who sat at his desk. He had been studying plans, but had abandoned them to admire his wife.

"Darling," her mother said, "look at this lovely new dress Papa has bought me."

"Why Mama, it is beautiful!" Gina exclaimed. "Such a gorgeous rich, red velvet."

"It seems as though I will have to buy some rubies to go with it," Papa said, grinning.

"You spoil me, my love," his wife told him tenderly.

"And what shall I buy you, my dear?" Samuel Wilton asked his daughter.

"Nothing Papa, you buy me too many things," she replied, kissing him on the forehead.

"That is one of the pleasures of money," he declared, with a happy sigh. "A man can treat his ladies. What shall I get you, my pet?"

"Nothing, Papa," she repeated firmly.

Gina knew that her father was an extremely wealthy man who could have afforded anything she asked for. For that very reason, she was reluctant to ask for a great deal. She was very much her mother's daughter, reared in vicarage standards.

Starting as a small builder, Samuel Wilton had progressed until he had a very large firm. From there he had gone on to speculate in the railways that were fast covering the country and made a huge fortune.

Gina had told John that he was a tradesman and insofar as a builder was a tradesman, that was true. But he was a tradesman writ very large indeed.

His enormous wealth had made him a man of distinction, mixing with other men of power and influence. He could have bought himself a title, but had simply never bothered to do so. At heart he was a simple man who had married a vicar's daughter and ran his life according to her strong principles.

He was rather in awe of his wife, knowing that his intellect did not match her own. He was in awe of his daughter for the same reason. And his love for these two women filled his world.

"Did you have a good day at the castle?" her mother asked.

"Yes, thank you Mama. And Lady Evelyn has invited me to stay for a while, so tomorrow I will be going back."

"Aiming to become a Duchess now?" asked her father, his eyes twinkling.

"Certainly not!" Gina snapped at once. "I am interested in the castle, as I told you last night."

"I know, I know, and the castle needs money. Or rather the Duke needs money."

Papa grasped her hands, his eyes alight.

"I know what, my pet. Shall I buy you the Duke?"

"Samuel!"

"Papa! How can you?" Gina was almost in tears. "What a terrible thing to say."

The good-hearted man looked blankly at the outrage of his wife and daughter.

"What's this? What did I say that was so dreadful? Eliza, my love, what did I say?"

"It was disgraceful," his wife told him severely.

"Why? Why?"

"Naturally our girl wishes to marry only for love."

"Well, she can love him, can't she? Best thing if she does. She will get a better bargain that way and if there's one thing I do know about, it's how to strike a good bargain."

Both his womenfolk covered their eyes at this vulgarity. Knowing that he was getting in deeper, but not too certain how, he blundered on,

"Besides, he is a handsome young fellow."

"You know him?" Gina asked, uncovering her eyes.

"Never met him."

"Then how do you know he is handsome?"

"Because you as good as said so last night."

"I never mentioned his looks."

"Not in words, but your eyes shone whenever you spoke of him."

"I deny it," Gina said fiercely. "He is nothing to me. *Nothing*! Do you understand?"

"Very well, my pet. There is no need to deafen me."

"Please understand that my concern is only for history."

"But you can concern yourself with history here," Samuel pointed out. "When that curate came round trying to whip up interest in saving the village wishing well, you took no interest beyond a donation. Of course, he wasn't handsome – "

"Papa, if you say another word I shall leave the room," Gina asserted fiercely.

"All right, all right. Dear me, it seems that everything I say is wrong."

"Besides, you do our girl an injustice," his wife assured him. "She is intellectual and high-minded. She would never be overly swayed by a young man's beauty or appearance."

"Then she is different to every other girl in the world," Samuel defended himself robustly. "Very well, I will say no more. Except this. Gina my dear, if you should change your mind, I could manage a dowry of about a quarter of a million and surely that would get the Duke out of his difficulties?"

Gina stared at her father, aghast.

"*I would rather die!*" she cried passionately.

Then she ran from the room, leaving Samuel staring after her in total bewilderment.

That night, when her maid had helped her out of her clothes and into her silk, embroidered nightgown and was brushing her hair, Gina suddenly said,

"It's all right, Bertha. You can go to bed now."

The maid bobbed and vanished. Gina looked at herself in the mirror.

'I would rather die,' she murmured. 'Did I do wrong in not telling him I am an heiress? Surely not. If he only wanted me for my money, I could not endure it.'

A tear trickled down her cheek.

'And I don't know why I am crying,' she sniffed. 'There is nothing to cry about. Nothing at all.'

*

John was in a testy mood the following morning. Breakfast had been made hideous by Drusilla's conviction that all problems were now solved and they could all begin to live like Dukes.

In vain did John try to explain that the idea was only in the planning stage and that they were still a long way from success. Drusilla's feather-brain had room for only one idea and it was invariably the one that suited her.

"You will give me a really grand ball, won't you?" she demanded of her brother.

"Whatever for?"

"For my coming out. How can I be a *debutante* without a coming out ball?"

"Why should you want to be a *debutante* if you are already planning your wedding?" he asked caustically. "A girl who has snared a man called Scuggins has surely nothing left to wish for."

Drusilla put out her tongue at him.

After breakfast John tried to do some work with his secretary, but what he discovered of the accounts only depressed him even more.

With one ear he was listening for the sound of Gina's arrival. When he heard the crunch of wheels he ran out to greet her.

Gina was leaning out waving to him and beaming.

He gave her a bright smile, feeling thoroughly confused. It was delightful to see her. Too delightful, he told himself. She was a terrible girl with advanced ideas of which he thoroughly disapproved. But she was also mysteriously bewitching and her visit was going to be a trial of both his nerves and his feelings.

He opened the carriage door and she immediately jumped down, seizing his hands in hers.

"I have some wonderful news to tell you," she said. "Wait until you hear it."

John waited hopefully. Gina's eyes were shining.

"I know an heiress," she declared.

"What?"

He could not believe his ears.

"She is enormously rich, and just what you need."

"Gina, we discussed this before, and I told you – "

"Oh, but I am not asking you to do anything dishonourable," she said fervently.

"A marriage for money sounds fairly dishonourable to me."

"Not if it is made for love."

"How can I be in love with her if I don't know her?"

"I will take care of that. The thing is, she is very pretty and charming, so you can fall in love with her and marry her with a clear conscience. That way you will get a better bargain."

"Get a – ?"

"I learned that from my father, because if there is one thing Papa does know about, it is how to strike a good bargain."

"I am going mad," said John faintly. "Any moment now I will start seeing visions or addressing people who don't exist. I find it hard to believe that you actually – *stars above!*"

"You don't think it's a good idea?" she asked anxiously.

"No, I do not think it's a good idea."

He could not have said why her eagerness to marry him off should trouble him so much. In theory he should be pleased, since it meant that she herself was certainly not setting her cap at him. He could simply dismiss the moment they had shared in the keep.

But somehow he did not want to do that.

"Who is this girl?" he asked.

"Oh – just an heiress."

"Just an heiress. There are so many, aren't there?"

"There aren't many heiresses as rich as this one and you would do well to consider her."

"You had better tell me her name, so that I can give her a wide berth."

"In that case her name doesn't matter," Gina replied stubbornly. "I'll warn her off you. I will tell her you are pig-headed and rude and – "

"Just tell her that I won't marry her," John interrupted wildly. "That will be quite enough, you dreadful girl."

Lady Evelyn came out onto the step in time to hear this last pronouncement.

"John dear," she murmured, "please remember your manners. Gina, how nice to see you. Come inside and see your room."

She swept their guest away, casting a reproachful look back over her shoulder at her son.

As the two women moved further into the house, Gina's plaintive voice drifted back to him,

"I fear I may have offended your son, ma'am. Such terrible things he says to me."

And his mother,

"Ignore him my dear. It is perfectly fatal to take the slightest notice of anything a man says or does."

John breathed hard, wondering how long it would be before he murdered Miss Wilton.

CHAPTER SIX

Pharaoh appeared on the step with a young man of mountainous proportions, whom he directed to start carrying in Gina's baggage. He explained himself slowly and with lots of gestures and the young giant nodded ponderously to show that he understood.

"Who is he?" John demanded of Pharaoh.

"His name is Harry, Your Grace. A sweet natured lad, but – " he gave a shrug. "Shall we say, not equipped to make his own way in the world?"

John needed no further telling that Harry was a lost sheep. He was beginning to understand that almost nobody else would work at the castle. Tennison, the butler, was still there, but apart from him John had seen nobody that he recognised.

Pharaoh added,

"Harry takes care of the kitchen garden, Your Grace. The vegetables he grows are a wonder to behold. Cabbages, potatoes, leeks, onions, herbs – "

"The vegetables we had last night were excellent."

"I will tell him you said so. He will be very pleased."

"Pharaoh, are there any more people that I don't know about?"

Pharaoh nodded.

"A few in the kitchen, Your Grace, and the stables."

"A few? How many?"

Pharaoh made a vague gesture.

"One or two – or maybe three."

"How many is that?" John persisted.

"Well – " Pharaoh made a vague gesture. "It's hard to be sure – exactly – but – "

"A few," said John, who was beginning to realise that he was not going to win this one.

"That's right," Pharaoh exclaimed. "A few. Oh, yes, and there's a couple who grow the loveliest flowers. Did you notice the flowers on the table last night?"

"Yes, my mother mentioned them most particularly. I was afraid that they had been sent in at great expense."

"Oh, my goodness, no. Culled from Your Grace's own garden."

"But they are magnificent. I didn't think we were capable of anything so beautiful."

"The horse manure is very useful."

"Horse manure? Do we still have enough horses to make a difference?"

"Not really, but Harry obtains the extra by doing a day's work on the local farms. He is much in demand on account of his strength."

"So he works for other people and gets paid in manure, which he brings back here and puts on my gardens?"

"On the castle gardens, Your Grace," Pharaoh corrected him gently.

"But the castle does not pay him anything for his work."

"He gets food and shelter, neither of which he could organise for himself. The castle is his refuge, a place where he finds the kindness the outside world would never give him."

"And my uncle was kind to him?"

"Yes, Your Grace. But *you* are the Duke now."

The implication was clear. Personalities did not matter here. *The Duke is dead. Long live the Duke.* And long live his responsibilities to those weaker than himself. Long live the castle that provided shelter to the poor and helpless.

It occurred to John that Gina would have understood all this. In fact, everything Pharaoh had said was a living proof of her view that the castle belonged to the whole district, which needed and depended on it.

Pharaoh picked up a bag and was about to turn away, when something stopped him.

"Visitors, Your Grace," he said, pointing to the gate tower, through which a carriage was rumbling.

John followed his finger and saw a very welcome figure stand up in the carriage, hailing him.

"Ahoy there! Anybody at home?"

"Well, I'll be – !" John exclaimed, a pleased grin breaking over his features. "By all that's wonderful. Benedict!"

His friend jumped down and rushed over to him with arms outstretched. Next moment the two young men were clasping each other exuberantly.

"I didn't hope to see you for days!" John exclaimed.

"I didn't think to get away for days, but when I arrived I found the house empty, the whole family having departed for a holiday by the seaside. Since I was coming from the seaside I found this slightly ironic. We may even have passed on the road. I left instantly and here I am."

"You were never more welcome, old fellow. I need your moral support badly."

"You sound like a drowning man."

"Going down for the third time, I can assure you. Come inside."

He went in immediate search of Sonia and Imelda, who did not let him down. Having contrived chambers fit for Gina and Drusilla, they scurried around and prepared something acceptable for Benedict. It was a little rough and ready, but to a man who had recently spent weeks on a ship it looked comfortable.

"I cannot tell you how glad I am to see you," John enthused fervently, when they were alone. "I am living in a madhouse, under the thumb of the most extraordinary female you ever met."

"Tell me everything," Benedict urged him.

*

In her own chamber Gina was finishing her unpacking, wondering if she had taken leave of her senses.

It had been an inspiration of the moment to tell John that she knew a great heiress, but on reflection, it was an inspiration that she should have suppressed.

However things had not gone too badly. His reaction had been in every way satisfactory and she had avoided giving this wealthy damsel's name, which would have been difficult, as she did not exist.

Drusilla descended on her wanting to gossip about the frivolities that occupied her thoughts these days. It took time to convince her that Gina was here to work seriously. After accepting that fact, she regarded her oddly, as though Gina had descended from another planet.

But, however frivolous she was, Drusilla had shrewd eyes where feminine finery was concerned and she did not miss the fact that Gina's clothes were created from the best materials. Her gowns were not fashionable, but her underwear was made of the softest linen, delicately embroidered.

"Have you ever been to London?" she asked, lounging on Gina's bed.

"Oh, yes, my parents took me there last winter. We had such a wonderful time, going to the Opera and seeing Shakespeare."

Drusilla made a face.

"But didn't you go to any balls?"

"One of Papa's friends gave a dance for his daughter and we did attend."

"But didn't your father give you a Season and a coming out ball?"

"Why should I want one? Seasons are for ladies in High Society, like you. I expect you will be having a ball soon."

"If I can persuade my mean brother to give me one."

Gina made no reply. She seemed struck by some thought that held her still, musing. Slowly she sat down on the bed, still lost in thought.

After trying to attract her attention Drusilla gave up in disgust and flounced out.

At last Lady Evelyn appeared, wanting to know if she had everything she wanted.

"I am very happy with my room, thank you, ma'am. All I want to do is get to work, so I think I will join Mr. Faber in the library."

"I will have refreshments sent to you there."

Suddenly she looked directly at Gina and said softly,

"Dear Gina, do you think it will work?"

"I don't know ma'am. That is – if you mean – "

Lady Evelyn met her eyes.

"You know exactly what I mean. I have done my part by inviting you – "

Gina giggled.

"He wasn't pleased at that, was he, ma'am?"

"Oh, never mind him. I am trusting you to win."

"I will do my best, ma'am."

Descending to the library, she found Ambrose going over lists. As she sat down Sonia appeared with the refreshments.

As a special mark of attention Lady Evelyn personally brought in the coffee and sandwiches.

"I hope I am not disturbing you, Mr. Faber."

"Not at all, ma'am."

He rose quickly to his feet and helped her with the cups, smiling. When they were finished he escorted her to the door and held it open as she passed through. Lady Evelyn gave him her most dazzling smile before disappearing.

Catching Gina's interested eyes on him, Ambrose coughed awkwardly. He was blushing.

"Lady Evelyn is so lovely, isn't she?" Gina asked.

"A most gracious lady. Shall we have our coffee and then return to work? I have just made a start on the invitations."

"Oh, dear, have you written many?"

"Only a few. I thought you would be pleased."

"The fact is there might be a slight change of plan."

Ambrose gave her a quizzical look.

"How slight?"

"Well – "

The door opened and John strode in. One look was enough to show that he was exasperated.

"Sisters!" he said with loathing. "I wish Drusilla would understand that there is no hope of my giving her a ball."

"But you must!" Gina exclaimed.

"What?" He stared at her.

"That is absolutely what you *must* do."

"Gina, this is going too far."

"But don't you see, it is the perfect way of getting people together?"

"I thought we were just going to invite them to a reception?"

"We were, but this is much better. I have been thinking of it ever since Drusilla mentioned it this morning. Invite people to a ball and let them see the castle 'in action'.

"During the ball we show small groups around and then return them to the dancing. If you just invite them to ask for their money, it might be a little awkward, but if there is something else going on at the same time, it will be easier."

"It's a very good idea," admitted Ambrose.

John could see that this was true. But he had a practical objection.

"How on earth can I afford to stage a ball here?"

"I think it might be managed with some patching up," Gina said. "And it doesn't matter if the place still looks shabby, because that is the whole point."

"But I have no servants."

"You have Pharaoh and Jeremiah, and the twins, and Harry, and actually there are several more."

"Pharaoh has been telling me."

"And I am sure my parents will lend us one or two of their servants," she continued, concentrating on something she was writing.

"That is most kind of them, but I couldn't dream of leaving them without servants for the evening."

"But they will hardly notice it, since they will be guests at the ball," Ambrose put in.

Gina sent him silent thanks. She would have died rather than explain to John that her parents had enough servants to stock the castle twice over.

Drusilla was ecstatic at the news that she was to have a ball after all. But when they went to take a look at the ballroom everyone fell silent with dismay. It was the worst room in the castle.

"It's not fair," Drusilla cried. "I will have a ball, I will!"

"But my dear, what can we do?" Lady Evelyn asked. "The only other room big enough is the great picture gallery."

"Then why don't we take a look at that?" Gina suggested.

To everyone's relief the picture gallery was still in reasonably good condition. It was warm and dry and only needed cleaning to make it usable.

There were vacant places on some of the walls, where pictures had been sold.

"And the ones that are left are not valuable," John observed. "Family portraits, painted for vanity, of no value to anyone but us."

"These are your ancestors?" Gina asked, taking a keen interest.

"This one is supposed to be Guy le Chester, painted in the days before artists used perspective."

"Is that why he seems to have two eyes on the same side of his face?" Gina asked, chuckling.

"No, I think he got that way in battle. He was a ferocious warrior by all accounts. And this Knight on a white horse is Baron Franken Chester."

"Ah," Gina sighed. "That's better!"

"The family was given an Earldom by Henry VIII and a Dukedom by Charles II. They supported him against Cromwell and even supposedly let him hide in the castle when he was escaping to France. When he gained the throne he rewarded them with the highest title in his power. This is the first Duke, Lionel. Splendid fellow, isn't he, in that full wig?"

"Very handsome. No wonder he had all those mistresses."

"What was that?" John asked, wondering if he had heard aright.

"The story is that he had a different mistress in every single tower of the castle and his wife never discovered any of them."

John stared at her, speechless.

"Mind you," Gina went on, "I should think she probably *did* know."

"Really?" John said in the most discouraging tone he could manage.

"A man should not assume that a woman knows nothing just because she says nothing."

"Would you like to see any more pictures?" he enquired frostily.

"Yes, please."

But the next picture caused him even more problems.

How, he wondered, had this outrageous creation ended up in the middle of these virtuous family portraits?

It showed several females, not so much clothed as draped, reclining on sofas. One was playing a lyre, one was looking into a mirror. The rest were being primped by attendants.

"Never mind that one," he said hastily.

"But I am fascinated by it. They are odalisques, aren't they?"

"Yes," John said, with a wild note in his voice, "they are odalisques."

"And you are wondering how I know what an odalisque is. It comes from having a classical education, I am afraid."

"You mean," he said carefully, "that you actually know what – I mean – "

"An odalisque is a concubine, a lady of the harem, trained from early years to think of nothing but what pleases her Master. Poor creature."

"I don't see that at all. They lived in pampered luxury."

"There is no luxury in the world that could compensate for the boredom of such an existence. Yes sir, no sir, three bags full sir. No man could possibly be worth it."

"You are probably right. Shall we continue? This gentleman here – "

"Did you meet any odalisques in your travels, John?" Gina asked impishly.

"This gentleman here is the third Duke," he persisted determinedly.

To his relief he saw his mother advancing on him.

"This will do wonderfully," she exclaimed.

"Oh, I can see me now," Drusilla sighed, "waltzing to the sound of violins, all eyes upon me – "

"I will get to work straight away," Gina said.

The rest of the day was taken up with invitations to a grand 'coming out' ball, given by the Duke of Chesterton for his sister Lady Drusilla. Since people were now being invited from far and wide the date was put back a week.

"How delightful," sighed Lady Evelyn. "Your brothers

will be home from school by then."

"What?" John and Drusilla spoke with one dismayed voice.

"They will be here just in time. Isn't that delightful?"

Admirably concealing their delight, John and Drusilla competed with each other to explain why the idea was simply impossible.

"Mama, if you think I am going to have those two little fiends at my coming out ball – "

"Things are quite bad enough, Mama, without – "

"But my dears," Lady Evelyn placated them, "what else can we do? We cannot hold the ball earlier, because there won't be time for the invitations to reach the farthest guests. I am sure Timmy and Roly will behave like little angels."

Having thus disposed of the problem to her own satisfaction, she floated away, leaving John and Drusilla, for once in harmony looking at each other aghast.

The argument was revived over dinner and was still simmering when the family gathered in the drawing room later that evening. But there was nothing to be done, so John reverted to his chief worry.

"The more distant guests will have to be accommodated for the night," he said. "So it becomes vital to patch this place up. I don't know if we can do it."

"It can be cleaned," his mother advised. "And, as Gina so wisely says, we want people to see the place looking shabby."

"Do we want them to fall out of the beds, which are collapsing?" John asked ironically.

"Calum could take care of that," Gina said. "I believe he is very good with his hands."

"I don't think I have encountered Calum," John observed.

"He works in the stables," Gina informed him. "Pharaoh says he is very good."

"And I can help," Benedict said. "I am a dab hand with a hammer and nails. In my home you had to be. I have mended my sisters' dolls, my mother's chairs, my father's desk."

"Splendid," John said robustly. "You can start on the beds in this place."

Benedict's arrival had proved a godsend. His beautiful manners and merry spirit had made him an immediate favourite with Lady Evelyn and when not talking to her he cracked jokes with Gina.

John was slightly annoyed to note that Benedict seemed much taken with Gina. After all, he had made his own disapproval of her plain.

A man could not trust his friends these days.

"What a smashing girl!" Benedict exclaimed to John privately later.

"Hmm."

"Just because you cannot make out what she is talking about, it doesn't mean that no other man can understand her," Benedict said with a grin. "Some of us are quite brainy, you know. Not brainy by her standards, of course, but she makes allowances, which I think is very nice of her, considering that she – "

"I take your point," John said frostily. "There is no need to elaborate."

It was not lost on John that Gina had been talking to Pharaoh, who was clearly confiding more in her than in himself.

This impression was confirmed when he subsequently discovered her having a conference with the twins, Pharaoh, Jeremiah and Harry. At least, it seemed like a conference to him. Gina insisted that it was nothing but a cosy gossip.

But whatever the word, it was clear that she was organising his house, the way she had organised the ball and would probably organise his life, if he let her.

But that he definitely would not allow.

The evening was drawing to a close. Drusilla, in a good mood now that she knew she was going to have her ball, was practising waltzes around the drawing room, gallantly partnered by Benedict.

Lady Evelyn and Ambrose were playing a card game. Imelda brought in the tea tray and Gina was just handing round the cups when there came the sound of the front doorbell.

Everyone stopped what they were doing and looked up, wondering who would come calling to the castle so late.

After a moment it came again, a heavy clanking sound that echoed right through the old building.

They looked at each other, puzzled.

Then they heard the sound of footsteps, the front door being opened and more footsteps approaching them. At last the butler appeared.

"There is a lady at the door, Your Grace," he announced loftily. "Her carriage has broken down and as it is too dark to travel further – she asks your assistance."

"Of course," John said at once. "Please show her in."

Tennison departed and returned a moment later, standing stiffly and bellowing,

"Miss Athene Wicks-Henderson."

Into the room floated a vision. There were no other words to describe her. In her early twenties, divinely fair, with a skin like peaches and huge blue eyes, Miss Wicks-Henderson came out of any man's dreams.

She wore a travelling dress of deep blue velvet with lacy ruffles down the bosom. At her throat twinkled a diamond.

But it was her beauty that held the attention of every man in the room. Such enchanting fair curls, dancing about her face, such depths to her blue eyes, such a provocative pout to her rosy mouth!

John, Benedict and Ambrose all stood staring in the most vulgar fashion. Even Tennison was transfixed, until recalled to his duties by a basilisk stare from another female who had entered behind the lady.

John stepped forward, clearing his throat.

"Good evening, madam. Chesterton, at your service."

The lady spoke and it was like the soft splash of spring water.

"Your Grace is too kind. Do forgive me for intruding on you at this late hour."

"Any hour that brought you to my house would be acceptable, madam," John managed to say gallantly. "Tell me how I may assist you."

"My carriage is broken and lies out on the road. And my coachman took a tumble and injured himself. Even if the carriage could travel, the poor fellow can go no further."

"Then you must bring him here, ma'am. I will send for a doctor and my own people will bring the carriage into the stables for repair. And, of course, my best accommodation is yours."

She gave him the full effect of her dazzling eyes.

"Sir, I do not know what to say."

"Only say that I may serve you and I have no more to wish for."

Then, before the startled eyes of everyone in the room, John took her hand and reverently kissed the back of it.

After that everyone managed to pull themselves together. John introduced Miss Wicks-Henderson to his mother, his sister and then to Benedict. And finally –

"May I introduce Miss Gina – "

"*Gina*!"

In the first sign of real animation that she had shown, the vision opened her arms and clasped Gina to her.

"Hallo Athene," Gina said. "Fancy seeing you."

She returned the hug, but seemed to be eyeing Athene with a certain wryness.

"You know each other?" Lady Evelyn asked.

"Athene and I were at school together," Gina informed her briefly.

"We were such friends," Athene gushed. "Gina used to help me with my work, because I am such a ninny. Ginny darling, it is so good to see you again."

She clasped Gina in another scented embrace, while John was left wondering at this girl who actually addressed the formidable Gina as 'Ginny'. For himself, he would never have dared, for fear of being struck by lightning.

It seemed that accommodating Athene for the night was a more complicated business than it had seemed at first.

The large, ferocious female immediately behind her was Mrs. Conway, her companion. Two smaller females who brought up the rear were a maid and a dresser.

Rooms would need to be found for them all, not to mention a coachman, a groom and two outriders. Miss Wicks-Henderson travelled in style.

"It might be simpler if Athene and Mrs. Conway joined me," Gina told John. "There is a second bed in my room and one in the attached dressing room."

"That's very kind of you."

Lady Evelyn made Athene sit beside her on the sofa while Gina made the necessary arrangements, shepherding Mrs. Conway and the other two servants upstairs to her room.

When accommodation had been found for the dresser and the maid, she returned to the drawing room, to find John sitting with Athene on the sofa, deep in conversation with her. From his expression he clearly admired her greatly.

Lady Evelyn was preparing to retire for the night. She personally escorted Athene out of the room, with Sonia and Imelda bringing up the rear like Ladies-in-Waiting. Benedict and Drusilla followed them.

Gina would also have followed, but John detained her with a light hand on her arm.

"So this lady is a school-friend of yours?"

"Yes. Of course, I was only there for two terms, but we became friends."

John looked at her keenly.

"Well, you gave me fair warning."

"Did I?"

"This morning. I take it that she is the great heiress that you promised me? But of course she is. You wouldn't neglect to check a detail like that. My dear Gina! Fancy managing to produce an heiress out of a hat. Is there no end to your talents?"

CHAPTER SEVEN

For a moment Gina could only gaze at John in outrage, as the monstrous implications of his words sank in.

"Are you suggesting that I – ?"

"Please don't waste time denying it. So her carriage broke down outside my door? My dear Miss Wilton that one had whiskers on when my uncle was a young man."

"You are extremely rude, sir."

"No, I am not. I am complimenting your organising skills. How you managed it in the time I cannot imagine. And I am exceedingly grateful to you."

"You are?" she asked in a hollow voice.

"You promised me that she would be 'pretty and charming', so that I could fall in love with her with a clear conscience. And you kept your word. I congratulate you."

"You – have fallen in love – with her?" Gina faltered.

"Not yet exactly, but I am in a fair way to it. After you ordered me to, I would not dare do less. Such eyes, such a mouth. And a fortune too. It seems too good to be true. You can positively assure me that she is enormously rich, can't you?"

"Yes," she snapped. "Her dowry will be a hundred thousand at least. And she is an only child, so there will be more to come."

He heaved a sigh of relief.

"Thank goodness. Think of the disaster if I fell in love and she turned out to be poor after all."

"Now you are making fun of me."

"Me? I wouldn't dare."

"After all those fine words about how you weren't interested in an heiress – "

"I didn't precisely say that. I said I wouldn't marry a girl I didn't love merely for her money, and you promised me a girl whose beauty would solve those problems."

Goaded beyond endurance, Gina stamped her foot.

"I have no fear of your falling in love, sir, since I do not believe you are capable of it."

"Now, what have I done to deserve that remark?"

"You forget that I know what you consider admirable in a woman. A pretty doll without an idea in her head, permanently prostrating herself before your masculine superiority."

"That's a slander."

"Oh, no it isn't! Your perfect woman is one of those odalisques in that picture, one who spends all day primping herself to look nice for her Lord and Master and never utters a word."

This was so perilously near to the truth that he checked himself on the verge of intemperate speech.

"I will not deny," he said after a moment, "that I think a woman's intellect is not the equal of a man's – "

"Hah!"

"I beg your pardon?"

"You said exactly what I would have expected you to say."

He met her eyes, glaring.

"I said what any reasonable man would say," he declared emphatically.

She glared back.

"You said what any ignorant man would say."

"Ah, now we are getting the truth. You think that all men are there to be trampled under your feet."

"I have never made any secret of it. What is more I would enjoy doing it," she threw at him.

"Including me."

"Especially you. Any man who has the unspeakable arrogance to talk that nonsense about male and female intellect needs to be reminded to '*cave quid dicis, quando, et cui*'."

She finished with a defiant toss of her head that clearly implied 'so there!'

John breathed hard.

"That remark was entirely unnecessary," he snapped.

"How would you know? You didn't understand a word."

"Don't be ridiculous. I studied Latin at Eton."

"So what does it mean?"

This, John felt, was hitting below the belt. Nobody expected a man to know Latin just because he had studied it.

"It means," explained Gina patiently, "beware what you say, when, and to whom."

"I am perfectly aware of that."

"Hah!"

"Don't start saying that again," he begged.

"All right, I won't. I will merely remark '*vir sapit qui pauca loquitur*' which, as you are doubtless aware, means that a wise man knows when to hold his tongue."

"And a wise woman, too. After all, you are the one who believes in the equality of the sexes."

"Then we understand each other," she said.

"I should think we do."

"You are beyond hope," she parried.

"Well, don't tell your friend, otherwise she might not marry me. And after all your hard work, that would be a shame."

"I think," Gina countered stormily, "that you are totally insufferable and I do not know why I am wasting my time."

"Perhaps you are trying to reclaim me?"

"That really would be a waste of time."

"True. I am beyond hope, remember."

John's lips were smiling but his eyes glittered. For some reason he was furiously angry, and it had driven him on to speak to her with cold, bitter irony.

How dare this domineering, interfering female back him into a corner, and practically march him up the aisle with another woman? Who did she think she was?

He thought of the moment they had shared in the keep, when their lips had nearly met. And all the time she had been planning to palm him off on someone else!

What did she have in her veins? Iced water?

He shuddered at the thought that he might have exposed his longing at that moment for her to laugh at him.

Then he thought of Athene's smile and his anger faded. At least there was one female in the world who acted like a woman. Maybe Gina had done better for him than she knew.

"Don't let us quarrel," he said, speaking more gently. "Give me your hand, and please don't be angry with me."

"How could I ever be angry with you?" she sighed, taking his hand. His tone had melted her.

He smiled.

"Very easily, if I don't obey your every command. Do not worry. I will do exactly as you have planned for me. I will flirt with your friend and do my best to fall in love with her – for the good of the castle."

Her temper flared again.

"John," she said through gritted teeth, "I did *not* arrange for her to come here."

"To be sure you didn't. This morning you spoke of an heiress that you were planning for me, and tonight an heiress turns up on my doorstep with the most unlikely story I have ever heard. If it wasn't you, it was the fairies. Only I don't believe in fairies."

"John – "

"You are quite right. Neither of us should admit to knowing too much. You did not arrange this. Let's leave it there."

He walked to the door and stood holding it open, leaving her no choice but to depart with dignity.

*

It took the combined efforts of her dresser and her maid to prepare Athene for bed, with her companion watching the whole business with glaring concentration.

Finally they all took themselves off and the two girls were alone.

"Athene, whatever are you doing here?" Gina wanted to know. "Does your carriage really need repair?"

"It does now," Athene confirmed with a giggle. "It took the coachman several attempts to damage it sufficiently."

"So it wasn't an accident?"

"Of course not. It was all Mama's idea. Ever since Papa made so much money, she has been set on finding me a titled husband. And when she heard that the young Duke had come home, she thought we should do something about it."

"Already? He has only been back two days."

"But news of such an event spreads like wildfire. Soon every heiress for miles is going to be having a breakdown just outside his door. Mama was determined that I would be the first, but I suppose you got here ahead of me."

"You think I – ? Certainly not. I am a friend of the family, invited to stay a few days to help renovate the castle."

"And you have no interest in the Duke?"

"None," she said shortly. "And I do not understand how you can you lend yourself to such a scheme."

"Oh, well, I wouldn't do it, of course, if he was old and ugly, but now I have met him I think he is very good looking and so charming. Don't you find him so?"

"No," Gina said gruffly. "I think he is insufferable."

"Really?" Athene's voice became theatrical. "Do you mean that, beneath his good looks, there lurks a darker side?"

"Definitely!"

"How very intriguing!"

"Be careful, Athene. He is no fool. Broken carriage, indeed!"

"You think he saw through me? No matter. As long as he realises how rich I am."

"Athene!"

"Don't be so shocked. We are not all bluestockings like you. You may float loftily above such mundane matters, but the rest of us have to go out and find husbands."

Her voice became low and conspiratorial.

"Between us, Mama is very cross with me for failing to bring Lord Renton up to scratch. Well, actually I did bring him up to scratch, but I could not make myself agree to his proposal. He smelled of camphor.

"To be fair to him, he was very nice about it. He told Mama that he had not proposed, so that she wouldn't blame me. But I think she suspects the truth and she told me that I must do better this time, or she would be very angry."

Athene paused for dramatic effect.

"So I really must make a success of this one," she finished.

"And the title is all you want?" Gina asked.

"Falling in love would be nice too, of course. And I think I could make him fall in love with me, don't you?"

She fluttered her eyelashes dramatically.

"Yes," Gina agreed shortly. "I do."

"But you are my friend," Athene said, eyes swimming with sincerity, "and if it were your wish, I would defer to your prior claim."

"I make no claim," Gina said. "You may marry him with a clear conscience."

She blew out the candle and tried to settle down to sleep, but her thoughts were in turmoil.

'I am so stupid,' she told herself. 'Why did I have to quarrel with him? After that moment in the keep when – well, *nearly*.'

She sighed.

'And fancy quoting Latin, and confirming all his worst prejudices about educated women. Why didn't I just keep quiet and say, 'oh, how wonderful you are'!'

But then she sat up in bed, thinking,

'Because I cannot do that. If that is the kind of silly scatterbrain he wants, then he is not the man for me. Athene will suit him admirably and everything is wonderful. I could not be happier.'

After that there was nothing to do but thump the pillow, by way of showing how happy she was.

The groom's injury proved to be of the useful kind that would need attention for several days, without making it necessary for anyone to fear for his well-being.

Miss Wicks-Henderson was thus free to enjoy the Duke's company without appearing heartless.

On the next morning he offered to show her the district on horseback to which she willingly agreed. Benedict also joined the expedition and it was he who insisted that Gina accompany them

"Indeed no," she said hurriedly. "I thank you, but I have a great deal of work to do."

"I am sure that Ambrose can manage the invitations without you," intervened John, who had overheard.

"I cannot leave all the work to him and your mother will also need my assistance."

"Mama has Pharaoh's help and a better major-domo I never saw. Also Sonia and Imelda are skilled in this kind of organisation. She will certainly not need you as well."

When Gina still hesitated, he came towards her with his most disarming smile, and took her hands between his. Benedict tactfully melted away.

"Are you still angry with me?" John asked.

"I do not see why you should say that," she replied gruffly.

"Because I behaved abominably last night. For some reason I was annoyed, although I cannot now remember why. And I made you suffer for it. Say you forgive me."

"There is nothing to forgive."

His smile grew a little whimsical as he said,

"But perhaps I have something to forgive. It was very unkind of you to quote Latin, when you knew I didn't understand. But I forgive you for being cleverer than me."

"Don't be absurd," she said, blushing. "Of course I am not."

"Why Gina, you are surely not conceding the superiority of my masculine intellect?" he teased.

"No, but I will agree that you have a lot to teach me about cunning," she retorted with spirit. "You don't mean a word of it. You are merely trying to put me in the wrong."

He raised his eyebrows.

"Is such a thing possible?"

She smiled back at him.

"I refuse to let you annoy me," she said. "Have an enjoyable ride."

"But I insist that you come with us?"

Firmly she shook her head.

"Is it settled?" Benedict asked, rejoining them.

"Gina refuses to accompany us," John told him.

"I have too much work to do," Gina repeated.

"Then I will remain and help you," Benedict offered at once. "How shocking of us all to go off on a pleasure jaunt and leave you to do all the work."

"Oh, but you must come with us, both of you," said Athene in dismay. "I cannot ride alone with the Duke." She lowered her eyes modestly. "It would not be proper."

"I will have a horse brought round for you at once," John told Gina. "And no more arguments."

She saw that he was determined and hurried away to change into her riding habit.

Normally she would have been pleased with the picture she presented in her olive green habit, but she could not think of that now. She would have given anything not to have to watch John flirting with Athene.

She knew her worst fears had been realised when she

saw her friend in a black broadcloth habit that showed off her elegant figure enchantingly. Both John and Benedict were regarding her with admiration.

All the horses in the castle stables were past their best, but the grooms managed to produce four animals of reasonable quality and they all rode off together.

It was a lovely day as they set out to explore the countryside. John and Athene cantered on ahead in animated conversation. Gina rode beside Benedict, whom she already liked a good deal. Benedict's father was a country parson and she, the grand-daughter of a clergyman, found no difficulty in talking to him.

Before long they discovered something else in common. Benedict's mother and sisters were women of learning, and the female education that apparently horrified John seemed natural to this young man with the round kindly face.

When Gina told him how she had fought John with Latin phrases, Benedict shouted with laughter, causing the two in front to turn and regard them.

"You were taking a risk, ma'am," Benedict spluttered, wiping his eyes.

"It annoyed him very much," she said in a tone of satisfaction, just loud enough for John to hear.

"I'll wager it did. John, what a very brave lady this must be to challenge you in Latin."

John ground his teeth. Why did the wretched girl have to tell that story?

He let his horse fall back until he was riding beside Gina, the better to hear what she was saying. There was no knowing what she might come out with.

Athene also fell back, so that she rode beside Benedict.

"We had a mild dispute," John said with a slight shrug. "But we resolved it, did we not?"

"Indeed we did," Gina agreed cordially.

"But what exactly did you say to him?" Benedict wanted to know.

Gina said lightly,

"I merely observed that '*cave quid dicis, quando, et cui*'."

"To which, of course, there can be only one answer," John put in quickly. '*Vir sapit qui pauca loquitur*'.

He carefully refrained from saying that this was the answer that he had actually given, an omission that Benedict duly noted.

"I am not sure of that," he said thoughtfully. "I would have thought a far better response would have been, '*Pessimum genus inimicorum laudates*,' Don't you agree, ma'am?"

"I was about to say exactly the same," Gina responded solemnly.

Since the words meant 'flatterers are the worst kind of enemies', Benedict was doubtful if this really was a more apt response. But if there was one thing certain in the world, it was that John had not the slightest idea, one way or another.

Unable to resist tossing a stick onto the fire, he asked innocently,

"Would that be your opinion, old fellow?"

"My opinion," John growled "is that no man should trust his friends."

He really should have known better. No sooner were the words out of his mouth than Benedict and Gina exchanged glances and drew breath to speak together.

"And if either one of you translates that into Latin, I will throw the pair of you into the dungeons," John growled before urging his horse forward, leaving the other two choking with laughter.

Athene joined him. She had been listening to the conversation, eyes wide.

"Latin sounds like such a difficult language," she sighed admiringly. "How clever gentlemen must be to learn it!"

He frowned a little at that. How much had she managed to understand?

"It is actually Gina who is the expert," he admitted reluctantly.

"Oh, surely not," she sighed with passionate fervour.

He considered trying to explain and thought better of it.

Besides, what did it matter? Athene's gloriously blue eyes were gazing at him.

Behind his back he heard Benedict and Gina laughing again and it took all his determination not to turn round to look at them.

After a while he made some humorous remark and Athene's delightful laugh was like the rippling of a brook. This time he did turn round to see if Gina was observing how well he was playing the part she had assigned to him.

But to his annoyance she and Benedict had fallen behind and were out of earshot. They were no longer laughing but, seemed deep in some conversation so interesting that they were clearly oblivious of all else.

Athene also noticed.

"Oh, dear!" she said prettily. "Do they not wish for our company?"

How charming was her modesty, he thought. It almost made up for the boredom of her conversation.

At that moment Gina laughed again, evidently at some witticism of Benedict's.

"Let us rejoin them," he said.

Together they turned their horses and fell into step beside the others. John had meant to arrange matters so that he and Athene were still riding side by side, but somehow things worked out differently and Athene finished up beside Benedict, and John was obliged by courtesy to ride with Gina.

"I am glad you are enjoying the ride so well," he said coolly.

"Very well indeed, thank you. Mr. Kenly is a most delightful companion."

"Does he speak enough Latin for you?"

"Fie, Your Grace! There is more to charming company than Latin."

"I am glad you think so."

"Mr. Kenly is also pleasant, generous and correct in all his thoughts and sentiments."

"Since he invariably agrees with you, you would be bound to think so."

"There is that to be considered," she said thoughtfully. "I hold it to be true that compatibility of mind is of the greatest importance and, alas, the hardest to find."

"You are too demanding, I think. If we all go through the world searching for compatibility of mind, it will be a long and fruitless search for some of us."

She smiled. It was very faint, but to John's eyes it seemed more mysterious than any woman's smile he had ever seen. He never knew what this girl was thinking, he realised. With Athene it was always quite obvious.

"Have I said something amusing?" he asked.

"No, something melancholy. You remind me how hard it is for me to find someone whose mind chimes with my own."

"Until last night I thought our minds were pretty much

in step," he replied. "But that, of course, was before you met Benedict."

"Ah yes! Such an excellent young man and one who talks equally well on all subjects."

"Good grief!"

They rode on for a while in a silence only broken by the twittering of birds, and the soft murmurs coming from Athene and Benedict.

"Surely," John resumed at last, "the mental compatibility you speak of cannot be essential in every relationship."

"In some it is more vital than others," she conceded.

"Human beings are more than minds, there is also charm and beauty to be considered."

Gina looked at him innocently.

"But I was speaking only of friendship."

To his dismay he found himself going red.

"So was I," he said hastily.

Raising his voice he called,

"Miss Wicks-Henderson, Benedict, we are nearing a charming spot with a stream. Would you care to dismount?"

The others expressed themselves delighted with this idea and a few minutes later they came to the place where trees overhung the water.

Then the gentlemen dismounted and prepared to assist the ladies. John turned to Athene, but Benedict was there before him, reaching up to place his hands about her tiny waist.

She put her own hands on his shoulders, looking down into his face with the same dazzling smile that John had seen turned on himself many times that morning. There was something automatic about it, he realised.

Then he saw that Gina, with that lamentable independence that characterised her, was preparing to dismount unaided and hastened to forestall her.

"Behave yourself," he told her, reaching up his hands. "Accept a gentleman's help, even if only for the look of things."

"The look of things can be very important," she responded demurely.

"Now what do you mean by that? You see, I do not trust you," he told her.

Her only answer was a laugh that shivered through him so thoroughly that he almost lost his grip. But he managed to recover himself, settle his hands on her waist, lift and lower her.

It was only for a moment that she slid down his chest, but it lasted forever, yet was over in a flash.

He was looking into her eyes and they seemed to be telling him something – if only he could be sure.

Perhaps her hands lingered on his shoulders for an instant. He was not certain. His head was spinning and all was confusion.

Benedict's voice seemed to come from a great distance.

"What a delightful place, old fellow. Is this still part of your land?"

"Er – yes – yes, we are still on my land."

Reluctantly he released Gina. She turned away from him at once, leaving him standing there, breathing hard.

The horses drank eagerly from the stream, while the ladies picked flowers and the gentlemen hovered solicitously around them.

"Such pretty flowers," Athene exclaimed. "How lucky you are, Your Grace, to have an estate that is so beautiful. Your Grace?"

John was staring into the distance.

"You are right," he said hastily. "It is, potentially, very beautiful."

"Oh, surely not potentially, but actually," Athene gushed. "I feel sure that it is perfect just as it is."

"You are very kind, madam, but it is far from perfect. Much needs to be done."

"You are right, of course," she conceded instantly. "Gentlemen understand these things. I am afraid that we poor, ignorant females allow ourselves to be distracted by trivial diversions."

He gave her a forced smile.

It was hard to concentrate on Athene when he was straining to overhear what Benedict and Gina were saying. But he forced his mind away from them and walked with Athene beside the stream.

"Did you know Miss Wilton very well when you were at school?" he asked, picking a flower and handing it to her.

She accepted it with a teasing smile of thanks.

"Oh, we were the best of friends for the little time she was there. We had a lot in common, being both only children and both rather isolated."

"Isolated? Why was that?"

"Most of the other girls came from titled families, but our fathers had invested in railways, so they looked down on us as tradesmen's daughters."

"Railways?" John echoed.

It was common knowledge that there were vast profits to be made in the railways that were springing up everywhere. The result was a girl like Athene with no title but money enough to buy a dozen of them.

"Railways," he said again. "I thought Gina's father was a builder."

"I suppose you might say that," Athene agreed thoughtfully. "I believe he started in a small way, but he has a huge firm now, and he made so much money that he invested in railways and made even more. He is reputed to be a millionaire."

"What?"

John's exclamation was under his breath and he hoped that Athene did not hear him.

What he had just heard was terrible.

Gina was the only child of a hugely rich man. In fact, she was a great heiress.

She had advised him that he needed an heiress.

But, far from attempting to fill the place herself, she had thrown another rich girl into his path.

She could hardly have said more clearly that he did not interest her.

He remembered when he had lifted her down from her horse, the heady excitement that had filled him, the sensation of holding magic in his arms.

She could have turned that moment into a kiss with a look, a smile. But he had detected no encouragement from her.

And the reason was obvious, he realised with dismay. He was being plucked, tied, trussed and served up like a turkey to another woman.

CHAPTER EIGHT

In the following days the castle began to hum. Gina was making a detailed inspection of every room, accompanied by Sonia and Imelda, who seemed to function as her *aides-de-camps*, taking notes of her ideas and scurrying around to carry them out.

John felt moved to protest.

"Gina, you are here as a guest. I cannot allow you to do the work of a housekeeper."

She seemed to consider this remark seriously.

"Very well. I will hand the work over to whoever you name."

That brought him to a standstill. There was nobody with Gina's organisational skills, except possibly Pharaoh and he was already fully occupied.

These days it was hard for John to know how to talk to her. The discovery that she had rejected him as a possible husband at the outset, even though he was officially unaware of it, was a blow to his pride.

At first he refused to admit that more than his pride was damaged, but as he thought of the sweetness of their friendship and what might have been, he discovered an ache of unhappiness.

Now more than ever it seemed pleasant to talk to her, but he had to make excuses to do so. Luckily their various duties in planning the ball gave him many opportunities, but it was always he who sought her out and never the other way round.

She had withdrawn altogether from the business of sending out the invitations. Ambrose had suggested that, as Lady Evelyn was to be the hostess, he could work just as well to her direction. Gina had agreed to this with relief.

So the invitations went out far and wide and almost at once the acceptances began to pour in. As Athene had predicted, the news of the young Duke's return had spread like wildfire. No family with a daughter to marry off, whether she be titled or moneyed, wished to miss the chance.

Lost sheep began appearing everywhere, although John saw few of them because they scuttled out of his sight at every opportunity. They were not afraid of him, but he was still unknown to them.

Their major task now was cleaning the picture gallery, which, like so many other chores, was under the direction of Pharaoh.

John came to inspect the work in progress and walked up and down silently, surveying the great room which looked better than it had, but still had one dismaying flaw.

"Is there something worrying Your Grace?" Pharaoh asked.

John stopped in his pacing and indicated the walls.

"It is a pity that my uncle had to sell so many of his pictures," he sighed. "It leaves great bare patches on the walls of a lighter colour than the rest. I know that people are supposed to see that the castle is in a poor way, but still – "

Pharaoh nodded sympathetically.

"It's a matter of pride, Your Grace. You want them to know in theory, but not see in practise."

"Exactly. But what can we do?"

"We could bring out some of the pictures that are in storage. The late Duke used to hide away the ones he didn't like."

"I don't blame him. Many of them are rubbish, but they will be useful now. Where are they?"

"In the attic."

Together they climbed to the upper floors where, by the light of a lantern, Pharaoh showed him a room packed with pictures, wrapped in brown paper, leaning against the wall. Together they began to unwrap them.

Most of them, as John had said, were rubbish, painted by indifferent artists.

"My grandfather considered himself a connoisseur," John said, trying not to wince at one particularly hideous example.

"Did he, Your Grace?" Pharaoh echoed. "Did he, indeed?"

His carefully blank tone revealed his opinion better than words could have done.

"And he knew nothing about the subject. I believe he squandered a fortune on poor pictures, most of which he had mistaken for Old Masters. He would bring them home, have them valued and then realise his mistake. But he wouldn't admit it. Too stubborn. And they still went up on the walls."

"Shall we put them back up for one night, Your Grace?"

"Yes, it's better than bare patches. I will leave it to you to decide which. But not that one," he added quickly, glancing at a large picture and then away again.

Pharaoh studied it.

"It's very – full of action, Your Grace," he said. "Unfortunately the artist had no skill in painting figures."

"I guessed that even as a child," John said with a

shudder. "I remember my grandfather telling me that it was called the *Crossing of the Rubicon*. I think this figure here is meant to be Julius Caesar. Or it might be a donkey."

He added with wry self-mockery,

"Perhaps Miss Wilton could tell us. Her classical education was far superior to mine."

"Did I hear my name?" came a voice from the door.

Gina appeared, her clothes covered in a vast grey apron and a smudge on her nose. She looked enchanting, John thought.

"We were choosing some pictures to hide the gaps on the walls," John told her, offering his hand to help her pick her way through the debris.

"That one?" she asked, aghast, indicating the picture which Pharaoh was still holding.

"No, I promise you."

"What is it meant to be? It looks like a herd of cows fighting in a quagmire."

"It is the *Crossing of the Rubicon*. That is Julius Caesar."

"You will never get anyone to believe it," she said firmly.

She began to giggle, sitting down on a box to enjoy the joke better. John joined in, simply enjoying the sight of her merriment. Pharaoh quietly lifted the great ugly painting and hauled it away.

Suddenly John's smile faded.

"Gina," he said anxiously, "this *is* going to work, isn't it?"

"Of course it is," she told him firmly. "Everything is going to work out well, you simply must believe."

"I do, but only when you tell me. You seem able to

116

make me believe anything. In fact, I realise now that that is what you do with everyone.

"I have seen you talking to Pharaoh and the twins, and some of the other lost sheep – those that don't run for cover when they see me."

"They only run because they are not sure they are safe here. They are afraid that you'll turn them out," she said.

"That would be very ungrateful of me, considering the work they are doing for me."

"Ah, yes, you need them now, but later, when you have money, you will probably want more conventional servants. Then you will send them away."

"Is that what they tell you?"

"Not directly. It is more something that I sense in the air."

"What do you tell them?"

She shrugged.

"I tell them how good-hearted and kind you are, but I cannot speak about your plans. I have no right."

"Good-hearted? Kind? It is not that long ago I was the most unspeakable, abominable – well, I forget the rest."

She laughed.

"I did not say you were not those things. I just said you were kind as well."

He grinned.

"Thank you. As for my plans, suppose I promised to do what you say?"

Regretfully she shook her head.

"You must not promise that to me.

"Why not?"

"Because I have no right to ask promises from you."

"But if I volunteer – "

"No, John," she said firmly. "Of course I would like to see you act kindly to them, but I have no doubt of that, because you are kind and generous. I trust to that. But there must be no promises because – "

"Because – " John prompted when she paused.

"Because one day there will be others in your life, who will have the right to ask promises of you. You cannot have divided loyalties."

She meant that he would have a wife, John thought, and telling him that she would never be that wife. In her sweet generosity, she was saving him from proposing to her and having to endure a rejection.

"Very well, no promises," he agreed quietly. "Except that I will say this. If you believe me to be kind and generous – though Heaven knows how you formed such an idea – then that is what I will be.

"I told you that it was your gift to put heart into people and for the rest of my life I will strive to live up to your belief in me. And that is something that you cannot make me unsay by any argument."

He thought that there were tears in her eyes, but in the gloom of the attic he could not be sure.

"I don't want you to unsay it," she told him at last. "You have told me that you will always be true to the highest in yourself and that is all I ask."

"Is that really all you want of me?" he asked, a little sadly.

"But of course. What more could I possibly ask than that?"

"Nothing, I suppose. I think – "

It took a moment for him to find the courage to go on, but when he saw her beautiful, earnest eyes on him he felt impelled to say the rest.

"I think, when I marry, my wife will owe you much."

"Oh, I don't think so," she said. "At any rate, you had better not tell her as much. Not if you wish to live in domestic harmony."

"I shall take your advice on that issue, as in everything," he said gravely.

"Which reminds me," she said, rising hurriedly, "I came to tell you that Lady Evelyn has received a letter from Athene's parents, accepting her Ladyship's kind invitation for her to remain here until the ball. Isn't that nice?"

"Wonderful," he agreed in a hollow voice.

*

With two days left to go, John's younger brothers came rollicking home from Eton. Timmy and Roly were twins, twelve years old and full of fiendish, zestful life.

Within an hour of arriving home they had released a pair of crows in the kitchen, creating mayhem and causing two scullery maids to have hysterics.

They followed this up by donning sheets and running up and down corridors making ghostly sounds until their brother threatened them with dire retribution. After which they gazed at him in wide eyed innocence.

Their mother praised their high spirits.

Drusilla said they should have been drowned at birth.

John said they were exactly like himself at the same age and he did not mean it as a compliment.

Benedict said they were 'great guns' and took them ratting in the barn.

Athene said she positively doted on them, but that was before they put a mouse in her bed, resulting in a shrieking fit that required all Benedict's efforts to comfort.

After that Athene maintained a deadly silence.

Gina got on well with them, because she always capped their blood-curdling ghost stories with even more spine-chilling stories of her own.

*

On the evening before the ball John took Gina aside, saying,

"Walk with me. There is something I wish to say to you."

For a while they walked in silence in the garden. Having made a start, John seemed to have difficulty deciding what he meant to say.

Gina waited with a heavy heart. She knew that after tomorrow she might never be happy again.

Then, as if their minds were intertwined, he said,

"After tomorrow, everything will be different."

"I know," she agreed sadly.

"Nothing in the castle or in our lives will ever be the same again."

Tomorrow night there would be the ball at which he would win support for the castle and probably announce his engagement to Athene.

"And that is why I wanted to talk to you now," he said, "before the wheel starts turning so fast that it cannot be stopped.

"Everything is due to you, Gina. It was your idea and I want the world to know what I owe you. When the names go up on the castle, one of them must be yours."

"I do not ask for that," she replied quietly.

"No, you never ask for anything for yourself, but people ought to know what you have done, not just now, but in generations to come."

"That is a long time. Things never work out quite as

we plan. All sorts of unexpected results will flow from what we plan tomorrow."

"I know, I have been thinking about that. Once a variety of strangers have paid for the upkeep of the castle, I shall have to let them come and visit it as often as they please."

"It will never really be a private home again," she concurred.

"But in six months time, when most of the work will have been completed, I shall invite you here as our Guest of Honour."

Gina laughed.

"I will remind you of that invitation in six month's time," she told him, "if we are still in touch."

"Why should we not be?" John asked.

"You may be bored with the castle and everyone in it," she said after a moment. "You will sail away, as you have done before, to visit castles overseas and find, perhaps, that people there are more attractive than those at home."

"No," he said seriously. "I shall never find that."

Suddenly Gina sighed and looked around her. The grounds were so beautiful in the golden light of the sunset.

"I am going to miss all this," she murmured.

"But you won't be leaving us just yet?" he asked in dismay. "You will be more needed than ever when people start putting money into the castle." He attempted a feeble joke. "Where would I be without my best administrator?"

"There will be nothing that Ambrose cannot take care of. He is scandalously under-used, you know. The work here is not nearly demanding enough for a man of his abilities."

"Then why does he stay?"

Gina was silent. She had her own opinion as to why

Ambrose stayed, but it was not for her to reveal the secret.

"You won't run away just yet, will you?" John begged.

"I will remain a day or two, but no longer."

She did not feel she could endure the celebrations of John's betrothal to Athene.

They were wandering under the trees now and from just above them came the sound of giggling.

John stopped and spoke loudly without looking up.

"If either of you are thinking of ambushing us, you can forget it now."

From high in the branches came groans of dismay.

"Spoilsport."

A piece of bark came tumbling down and fell at Gina's feet.

"That's enough!" thundered John. "How dare you alarm a lady."

"Gina isn't alarmed," came from the branches.

"She's not a spoilsport."

"Who said you could call her 'Gina'?" John demanded.

"I did," Gina said. "Don't be cross with them, John. There is no harm in them."

She smiled up into the branches.

"Perhaps you should come down now," she suggested.

They slithered to the ground at once and stood there, incredibly scruffy considering how spotlessly they had started the day, and looking up at their brother with an air of innocence that did not fool him for one moment.

He scowled at them.

"About tomorrow – " he said.

They stood to attention.

"And stop that," he commanded.

They saluted.

Gina covered a smile with her hand.

"And you just encourage them," John complained.

"No, I don't," she said at once. "They don't need any encouragement. And if you will talk to them like a Sergeant Major, what do you expect?"

"Whose side are you on?"

"Theirs."

The boys cheered and saluted again. One of them discovered something in his hair and tried to detach it to get a better look.

"I should leave it," Gina advised cheerfully. "It's only jam."

They both grinned at her.

"About tomorrow," John tried again. "You two will behave yourselves. You will be clean and tidy. You will speak only when spoken to and you will go to bed at the earliest possible moment. You will also refrain from introducing livestock, of whatever kind, among the guests."

"Their lives won't be worth living if you spoil all their fun," Gina objected.

"Now, scram, the pair of you!" John ordered.

Grinning, they ran away.

"I suppose it is time we went in too," John said reluctantly.

"Yes," she said wistfully. "It was such a beautiful sunset. I am glad we saw it."

Very tentatively he took her hand, wondering if she would rebuff him. But she did not, and they strolled hand in hand through the gardens and into the house.

*

Everything was ready. The house had been cleaned,

the kitchen garden raided of vegetables, the food had been cooked and the cellar stripped of drinkable wines. The stables were ready for an influx of horses and carriages.

But before the first guests arrived there was something that John was determined to do.

"Pharaoh," he called, "I want you to gather all the lost sheep together and bring them to the picture gallery."

He did not have to explain the term 'lost sheep' to Pharaoh, who understand perfectly and hurried away.

"What are you going to do?" Gina asked.

"Come with me and you'll see."

She followed him to the picture gallery. On the way they were joined by Benedict who silently asked Gina what was up and received the silent answer that she had no idea.

This was not strictly true. A hopeful thought was forming in Gina's mind, but if she was right it would be so wonderful that she did not dare to let herself believe it.

The musicians had not yet arrived and the picture gallery, now a ballroom, was empty. As the three of them entered, their footsteps seemed to echo.

"They should be here at any moment," John said quietly.

Soon they began to arrive, first the ones like Sonia and Imelda that the family knew. Behind them came the others, who existed in the nooks and crannies, hoping to live out their lives unnoticed, because they had always felt safer that way.

And how *many* of them there were, John thought with a sense of shock. Fifty? Sixty? And he had never known.

They were looking at him, some smiling, but cautiously. He was not the late Duke, who had made them welcome, but he had not sent them away and they were beginning to trust him.

For a moment he wondered how to say what was in his mind. Then he saw Gina's eyes on him. She was smiling as if to say that she knew he would do the right thing. And suddenly the right words came.

"It is so good to see all my friends together and to know that I have so many of you."

At once a ripple went over them. They were his friends. He had said so. They began to smile, not at him, but at each other, exchanging silent pleasure, sharing the good feeling. He had called them 'friends'.

He indicated for them to come closer and, carefully, they did so.

"I do not know how tonight is going to turn out," he told them. "With luck we may find enough money to restore the castle to glory and if that happens it will be your success, not mine.

"You have worked hard to help the family go on living here and to make this place presentable. Without you, it could not have been done."

He paused.

"If we do not raise as much as we need – "

They were all looking at him expectantly. Trustingly.

"If we don't get enough – then I promise you that we will continue here somehow. This is your home as well as mine. You have made it yours by your work and by your love. You may all stay here as long as you wish. You have my word on that."

There was an audible gasp from the crowd and then cheers of joy rang up to the roof as they vented their excitement, hugging and kissing each other. Tears of joy were flowing down the cheeks of just about everyone.

John saw this reaction with astonishment. He had known that they would be pleased, but this sudden glimpse of their desperation came as a shock. They had cared so much, been so afraid and he had not understood until now.

He had a sensation of almost terrified relief, as though he had narrowly avoided maiming a child. In his blindness he had so nearly caused a tragedy, but some power had guided him through.

Then he saw Gina and she too was weeping, although why she should weep he could not say. Yet, strangely, she looked happier than he had ever seen her.

He saw her open her arms to Pharaoh and be enveloped in his huge hug. Then the twins, Jeremiah, Harry. They all wanted to hug her, as though they knew that she had been on their side from the beginning.

And suddenly John felt lonely, because nobody was hugging him.

Of course, respect for his position would prevent them doing so.

But he still felt lonely.

Benedict too was beaming and overjoyed. He shook John's hand, pumping it vigorously.

"Well done, old fellow. You have done a wonderful thing. I knew you wouldn't really throw them out."

"That's more than I knew myself."

"No, no, you just talked that way. It didn't mean anything. Gina – " Benedict turned to find her beside him. "Isn't it wonderful?"

"It is the best thing that has ever happened," she said, her eyes shining. "John, I am *so* glad."

"Are you really?" he asked, wanting her approval more than anyone's.

"Of course I am. Just think what would have happened to them. They have nowhere else to go."

"That's not what I – Gina – "

But she vanished. An impromptu dance had started and somebody had whirled her away. Benedict followed, rescuing her from her exuberant partner and dancing with her himself.

John watched them, seeing how eagerly they were talking even as they danced and how they hugged each other again, as though in some secret understanding.

He turned away. He could not bear to see it.

Suddenly he found himself remembering the night he had docked at Marseilles and received the telegram that told him of his inheritance.

He had told Benedict then that he had been looking for something. He didn't know what it was, but it would be something different, something outside his own experience, that would make sense of the world.

But, with the title hanging round his neck, he had been sure that he would never find it.

"All hope is gone," he had said.

And yet, if he had had the sense to see it, that 'something' had been waiting for him when he stepped off the ship at Portsmouth and found a bright-faced eager girl, whose eyes were vivid with life and enthusiasm, who had wanted only to share her gifts with him.

But he had not had the wit to see it and the miracle had passed him by. Now he could see the truth, he could see that she was the one and only woman for him. But it was too late.

This time all hope was really gone.

CHAPTER NINE

But John knew that he could not allow himself to brood. At any moment the first guests would be arriving and he must be in position to greet them. These would be the ones who had come some distance and must be accommodated overnight.

"They are going to be on us at any moment," he told Pharaoh.

"Very good, Your Grace."

He began to urge the others to calm down and then to leave. In a few minutes there was only John, Gina and Benedict left.

"I still have some errands for Lady Evelyn," Gina said and hurried away.

"John," Benedict said, sounding awkward.

"What is it, old fellow?"

"Nothing, just – good luck. I know how important tonight is to you."

"More important than anything has ever been in my life," John replied.

"The thing is – a man doesn't always choose what happens to him – and what he does about it."

John frowned, alerted by a strange note in Benedict's voice. But then his brow cleared as he realised what his friend was really saying.

"He cannot choose where he falls in love, can he?"

"That's just it," Benedict said, relieved. "It can happen when you least expect it – like a bolt from the blue."

"Yes," John murmured. "I know."

So he really would have to face it, he thought. *Benedict and Gina.* He had watched it happen under his nose and only half understood.

Tonight they would announce their betrothal and he would smile and pretend to be pleased for them.

And he would never be happy again.

"The point is," Benedict was continuing with difficulty, "my father always preached that there were more things that mattered than human happiness and they should not be taken at someone else's expense. What do you think?"

John pulled himself together. He had promised Gina to stay true to the best in himself and now that he could do her a service, he would hold to that promise, whatever it cost him.

"What I think," he said, "is that there is too little happiness in the world and if you have the chance, you should take it. Does she love you?"

"Oh, yes, she says she loves me as I love her."

John winced, but tried to hide it.

"Good luck to you old fellow. Marry her with my blessing."

Benedict's round honest face shone.

"I say, that's wonderful. I had never hoped – thanks old chap."

He hurried away, leaving John standing alone in the echoing hall.

He tried not to think of Benedict rushing to Gina, taking her in his arms, celebrating their mutual joy.

And Gina, raising her beautiful eyes to the man she loved, never knowing that there was another man who loved her, although he had only discovered the depth of his longing too late.

It was all over now, except that it had never really begun. He had lost her, but she had never been his. And now he must learn to live without her.

A figure appeared at the far end of the gallery.

"John," Lady Evelyn called. "What are you doing loitering here? Guests are beginning to arrive."

"Very well, Mama. I am coming."

Goodbye to hopes of love, he thought, as he took his place beside his mother at the foot of the stairs leading into the downstairs hall.

They began to arrive, the Duke of this, the Marquis of that, Earls, Viscounts, Knights, Baronets. Lady Evelyn's performance was flawless. She greeted them all graciously and received many glances of admiration for her beauty.

There were sons, too, heirs to great titles, who eyed Drusilla with longing. She had no money, of course, but she was sister to a Duke and that could be as good as a dowry.

She returned their glances, her eyes lingering on handsome sons, who smiled back and begged her for dances as soon as they could get a private word with her.

She looked magnificent in the white gown of a *debutante*, with white rose buds in her hair and a pearl pendant about her throat.

Now the musicians were arriving, taking their place in the balcony above the floor where the dancers would soon be.

John walked upstairs to take a last look at the picture

gallery and stood listening as a violinist tuned up.

After a moment, Gina appeared and stood for a moment, also listening.

"Did you notice how delightful your sister looks?" she asked.

"Indeed. Let's hope this works and we will see off Arthur Scuggins."

"Poor man," Gina said, "you are very unkind about him."

"I intend to treat him with perfect courtesy. May I say that you look delightful?"

Gina was dressed very simply in a honey-coloured gown of satin and lace. A single strand of pearls encircled her neck and she carried an ivory fan.

"Thank you, kind sir."

"You must promise me a dance."

But she shook her head.

"Gina, are you saying that you will not even dance with me?"

"You will not have the time. Your whole evening will be filled with duty dances. And then, of course, you must spend some time on the main business of the evening, persuading people to help the castle."

"Oh, yes!" He gave a sigh.

"What is it, John?"

"Now that it has come to the point, I would give anything not to have to do it. If only I could find some way of saving the castle by my own best efforts."

He took her hands and spoke ruefully.

"I am an ungrateful dog to say such a thing, after all your hard work. Forgive me."

"But there is nothing to forgive," she said earnestly.

"Of course I always knew that you wouldn't do this if you had the choice. But there was no choice and I only wanted to find a way to help."

"And you have helped. Nobody has worked as hard as you or been so clever – no, not clever – brilliant."

"Brilliant?" Her eyes teased him. "And me a mere woman?"

"My dear, won't you forget whatever stupid words I may have said? I have learned so many things from you."

"Oh, yes," she said wryly. "I am an excellent teacher."

"You are a very great deal more than that and you know it. And if you are a teacher – you are the best kind, one who teaches by inspiring her pupils. You have inspired me to do what I must do tonight."

"I know you will do whatever you feel is right," she muttered.

In her heart she was sure that he was telling her that he had decided to marry Athene. After tonight he would be the promised husband of another woman and she had only herself to blame.

In a sense this moment between them was a kind of goodbye.

Her heart ached.

Above them the violinist had begun to play a soft waltz.

"If you won't dance with me at the ball, then you must dance with me now," John asked, holding out his arms.

She went into them and he began to waltz her gently about the floor, dipping and swaying in time to the music.

"Whatever happens tonight will be *your* success," he murmured. "Aren't you proud?"

Dumbly she shook her head. Tears glistened in her eyes.

He saw them and suddenly nothing could have stopped him kissing her. He bent his head and laid his lips against hers and found her as sweet as he had dreamed she would be.

For a delicious moment her soft, warm breath was against his mouth and he was in Heaven.

"Gina – "

And then the moment was gone. He saw her eyes, wide and horrified and felt her pull away.

"Gina – "

"No – no, we mustn't – "

She freed herself and backed away from him.

"Please John, this cannot happen – let us forget – we *must* forget – "

"Can you forget?" he asked her, almost angrily.

"I must – I must – "

Her voice floated back to him as she fled.

He followed her out into the corridor, then the main staircase, but she was running fast and all he could see now was a pale figure, vanishing into the gloom of another corridor.

Perhaps, he thought, she had run to Benedict, to tell him how shamefully his friend had behaved, only a short time after uttering generous words.

He was about to turn away when he became aware of Pharaoh gliding across the hall below. With him was a man he had never seen before. He was elderly, bespectacled, grey-haired and as thin as a rail, dressed in clothes that were neat but inexpensive, and he was hurrying along as though driven by some urgent purpose.

"Pharaoh," John called over the banister.

But neither of the men seemed to hear him and then they were gone.

And now it was time for the ball to begin and John must play his part.

More guests were arriving, among them Athene's parents, a large prosperous looking father, and a tiny shrewish woman with sharp eyes that saw everything, and made everybody feel uncomfortable.

Her glance raked her daughter up and down, as though demanding of Athene why there had not yet been an announcement.

John was charming to her, feeling sorry for Athene.

At the door Pharaoh called imposingly,

"Mr. and Mrs. Samuel Wilton."

A fine looking couple appeared. The man was tall and well built, the woman elegant in a red velvet dress with rubies set in gold surrounding her neck.

John saw Gina hurry up to them, hands outstretched in greeting.

"These are my parents," she said, drawing them closer and introducing them to John and Lady Evelyn.

While they were thanking their hostess for taking care of their daughter for the last two weeks, and being assured that Gina was the most delightful guest imaginable, John took the opportunity to study Mr. and Mrs. Wilton and immediately liked them.

There was a warmth and kindliness that emanated from them and the clear affection that united the three of them was one of the most attractive and enviable things he had seen for a long time.

He would have liked to engage them in conversation, but Drusilla was pulling at his arm.

"He's here," she cried excitedly. "My Mr. Scuggins is here."

"Then try to greet him calmly," he cautioned. "More

134

like a lady, less like a hoyden."

"I am a perfect lady," she replied haughtily.

Footsteps were approaching. In another moment the family would be treated to the appearance of *my Mr. Scuggins*. They all braced themselves.

The footman stood to attention and announced,

"Mr. Arthur Scuggins."

A shadow darkened the doorway. He was upon them.

To say that Arthur Scuggins was not what any of them had expected was to understate the case. His figure was tall, lean and elegant and he was dressed with perfect propriety.

He was about forty years of age and everything about him bespoke a quiet, serious man. The only sign of flamboyance was the diamond that glittered in his neck cloth. One glance at that jewel convinced John that Mr. Scuggins was as wealthy as Drusilla had claimed.

As he made his way across the floor towards them, John realised that the fat, elderly vulgarian he had been expecting had never existed outside his prejudices.

"Your Grace," he said calmly with an inclination of his head.

"Call me Chesterton," John said at once. "I believe I am much in your debt for your kind services to my sister."

He introduced his mother, who also thanked him profusely. Then he could turn his attention to Drusilla, and John was startled by the light that came into his eyes as he beheld his lady love.

How, John wondered, had his shallow, selfish, feather-brained little sister ever managed to attach this man?

Doubtless, the answer was her youth and beauty. Clearly Scuggins could do better, but as a good brother, it behoved John to make sure they tied the knot as quickly as possible.

The music began. He led Athene into the dance.
Benedict gave his arm to Gina, while Drusilla virtually
hurled herself at Arthur Scuggins.

But when the first dance was over, a demon seemed to
take possession of Drusilla. She did not dance with Arthur
Scuggins again, which was understandable at first, as she
had many duty dances to do.

But all of her dances were with handsome young men
with whom she flirted outrageously. As the evening went on
she passed from one to the other, laughing, teasing and
making coy overtures.

When Arthur Scuggins ventured to approach her, she
giggled and told him that she had far too many partners to
spare him another dance. His response to this was to bow
quietly and leave her.

"If you are trying to make him jealous you are being
very stupid," John told her fiercely when he could grasp her
for a moment.

"Who cares? You don't want me to marry him
anyway."

"That was before I met him. Now I begin to think he
is a sight too good for you."

She shrugged.

"I can do as I please. He won't say anything."

"Well, I will say that you are a little fool, and I am
ashamed of you."

She flounced off into the arms of another partner, a
man John disliked. He had cold predatory eyes and had
made certain that he danced with the wealthy Athene before
the penniless Duke's sister.

He looked around for Athene, but could not see her.
Her parents, too, seemed to be searching for her. Not finding
her, they approached John and her father cleared his throat.

"We were wondering when would be the best time for a serious talk, Your Grace."

"I will be delighted to talk with you, but first I must attend to urgent business. If you will excuse me."

It was almost time for him to gather his guests together and explain what was on his mind, and however reluctant he might be, he was briefly glad of it, since it enabled him to put off the moment with Athene's parents.

He looked for Gina, but was unable to see her either. Probably the two girls were somewhere alone, touching up each other's hair, which the dancing might have disarranged.

But she ought to be here. He hunted for her and at last realised that he would have to do it without her. He felt strangely abandoned.

*

Gina seldom danced, acting chiefly as a right hand to Lady Evelyn. And at some point in the evening she had noticed Pharaoh behaving strangely. He came and went at unexpected moments and was absent frequently.

When she next saw him, she took firm hold on him.

"Pharaoh," she said urgently. "Something is happening, isn't it?"

"Yes, madam."

"Can you not tell me what it is?"

"If you would follow me, madam."

He led her along dark corridors until they came to the room where he had been working. There she found Timmy and Roly, who had been officially sent to bed hours ago, full of excitement.

There was also a lean, grey-haired man with spectacles. He was peering through a magnifying glass at one of the pictures.

"Haven't changed your mind, have you?" Pharaoh

asked him.

"Oh, no, no, not at all," the man murmured.

"Miss Wilton," said Pharaoh, "allow me to introduce Jake Norris. He is an art expert. Do I say art expert? No. He is *the* art expert."

It was then that Gina noticed something different about the picture.

"Isn't that the *Crossing of the Rubicon*?" she asked.

"It was," Pharaoh answered. "Until I removed it."

"Removed it? How?"

"Cleaned it off and revealed the picture underneath. That's what Jake has been studying and he has made a discovery, haven't you Jake? Jake?"

"Eh? What?" Jake looked up, his eyes vague. "You know, this is really most interesting."

"You had better tell Miss Wilton."

So Jake explained. Gina listened with wide eyes and when he had finished she sat down as if the breath had been knocked out of her.

"Whatever will John say when he hears this?"

"He won't have to raise money tonight now," Roly piped up.

"He'll like that," Timmy added.

Gina took a deep breath.

"But it's too late," she said. "He is gathering everyone to make a start. What can I do? I cannot dash in while he's talking, drag him away and then leave him to go back and tell everyone he didn't mean it."

"But he should know about this discovery before he commits himself," Pharaoh pointed out.

The boys were looking at each other, their eyes gleaming.

"Would you like to hear a plan?" Timmy asked.

"What sort of a plan?" Gina asked cautiously,

"A deep, dark, devilish plan," Roly supplied.

"Yes, I think I might be interested."

They explained. When they had finished Gina said urgently,

"We must move fast."

"You'll have to talk to the others," Timmy said. "They won't do what we tell them, but they will for you."

"Let's get to work," she urged.

*

Down below, John had returned to the ball, silenced the orchestra and commanded the attention of the guests.

"I am sorry to interrupt your enjoyment," he began, "but I have something to say that I hope you will be interested to hear."

They turned to regard him, their faces full of attention and anticipation. John took a deep breath.

The moment had come.

"This is the first ball that has been held in the castle for nearly thirty years," he said. "One or two of you here now were here then and can remember what a fine place this was, in its prime."

Murmurs of agreement went around the gathering.

John paused for a moment. Then he added very quietly,

"Look at it now. What has happened? How is it possible that we could neglect anything so fine as this castle, which was meant to be cherished by us, our children and their children?"

He realised that there was absolute silence in the hall. Everyone was listening intently.

"How is it possible?" he asked. "How did it ever happen that the castle, which meant so much to our ancestors, should be in such a state as it is today? It is almost in ruins and unless we stop it, it will soon be just a pile of rubble and will be lost for ever."

Suddenly it was difficult for him to go on. The next stage was asking them for money and his pride held him back. It was vitally necessary, but now that the moment had come, he was reluctant.

Then, before he could continue, a strange noise floated through the gallery.

"*Whooooo – ooooooh!*"

Silence.

Everyone was looking around them, trying to work out what the noise was and where it had come from.

"It was probably the wind," John said. "As I was saying – "

"*Whooooo – ooooooh!*"

This time his audience looked around them more anxiously, frowning, baffled, beginning to become a little nervous.

"What is it?" asked an apprehensive young lady.

"Nothing, I do assure you," John answered, but he was interrupted by a shriek from the back of the crowd.

"I saw something."

"Where? Where?" everyone wanted to know.

"There! A figure in a white sheet. It's a ghost."

"Of course it isn't a ghost," John said, raising his voice to quell the hubbub that had been created. "We don't have any ghosts."

"Yes, we do," Drusilla put in. "There's the headless lady and the man who died on the gallows and – "

"Whooooo – ooooooh!"

"There it is," someone shouted.

"No – there."

"There's one over there!"

Under cover of the commotion John hissed into his sister's ear,

"If you say another word I will make you sorry you were born."

"It's not my fault," she asserted, all injured innocence.

"It's the fault of those two little fiends from hell who call themselves my brothers. I don't know what they are playing at but – "

"Whooooo – oooooooh!"

He stopped because his attention had been drawn to a sheeted figure standing motionless on the upper gallery. It was gigantic, evidently the spirit of some huge ancestor.

Or Harry in a sheet.

"Just what is going on," John muttered wrathfully.

Even as he looked, the figure began to move back, until it had vanished.

It was too late now to calm the crowd. Sheeted figures were running hither and thither from door to door. Ladies were beginning to scream and the men to shout. A riot was developing.

"Everybody – please – " he called.

Then he felt a hand plucking at his sleeve and he was being dragged irresistibly away, with no chance to object until he found himself right out of the gallery and the door closed behind him.

"I am sorry, John," Gina whispered, releasing him, "but I had to get you away before you could say any more."

"But I have got to say more. This whole plan – "

"May not be necessary after all."

"Whatever are you talking about?"

"I want you to come with me and trust me," she said urgently. "Come now."

Without waiting for his answer she took his hand and began to lead him quickly away.

"Where are we going?" he asked.

"You will see," was all she would say as she hurried along.

Higher and higher they went, until they reached the room where the pictures were stored. There they found Pharaoh and Jake Norris.

"Here he is," Gina told them.

"What is this all about?" John demanded.

"Tell him about the picture," Pharaoh said, rubbing his hands with glee.

Jake Norris looked up.

"You are – er – the Duke? The owner of the Rembrandt?"

"*Rembrandt*?" John echoed. "I don't own a Rembrandt."

"This picture isn't yours?"

"Yes, of course it's mine, but it is not a Rembrandt."

"Oh, dear me, yes it is. A very fine example of his later work. Quite incredibly valuable."

John stared at him.

"Are you quite certain of what you are saying?"

"Totally certain. As soon as my good friend – " he indicated Pharaoh, "notified me that he had discovered one picture beneath another and he thought it was a Rembrandt, I dropped everything and came straight here."

"You did that?" John asked Pharaoh. "But how did

you know?"

"I am familiar with various artistic styles," Pharaoh replied vaguely.

"Best forger in the business," Norris declared, not mincing matters.

"I don't care what he was," John said. "Is he right about this?"

"No doubt of it."

"And there are a couple of other pictures that I think would yield interesting results if I cleaned off the surfaces," Pharaoh added.

"Then you had better get on with it while I am still here," Norris said. "But this picture alone, Your Grace, will bring you a very considerable fortune."

"I know you were reluctant to take the final step to raise the money," Gina admitted. "We had to stop you before you went any further."

"So you thought of the ghosts?"

"Actually that was Timmy and Roly's idea. I went round our friends and persuaded some of them to help."

"Yes, I recognised Harry."

John sat down suddenly and dropped his head into his hands. When he looked up at Gina, his eyes were shining.

"Do you realise what this means?"

"Yes," she said eagerly. "You are saved. Oh, John, just think of it! *You are saved.*"

CHAPTER TEN

"Saved," John repeated in a dazed voice. "Saved."

"This picture will restore your family fortunes," Gina sighed. "You will be free to – to do whatever you like."

To do whatever he liked. Did she realise, he wondered, how ironically those words rang in his ears now that she had declared her love for another man?

He tried to force a smile. He had just found a vast fortune, but if she did not love him nothing seemed to matter very much.

"John, listen," she took his hands. "I think you should go downstairs now and talk to your guests."

"Good grief, yes! I have told them half the story. What shall I say now?"

"Tell them the other half, that you have just discovered a great picture that will solve your financial problems. Then invite them to share your joy."

"Yes, you are right. Come with me."

Together they made their way down and back into the picture gallery. The crowd was still there, calmer now, although they seized on his return.

"Whatever happened?"

"What were those terrible figures?"

"Do you really have ghosts?"

He faced them, calm but pale.

The words he uttered were the words Gina had given him. He was still too stunned to think up a speech of his own.

Most of the guests saw only the tale with the happy ending and cheered him, kindly and enviously. Only a few of them could guess at the undercurrents swirling around.

Lady Evelyn regarded her son with a smile but also a touch of anxiety, as though wondering what would happen next. She had been watching him for the last couple of weeks, hoping against hope that she was reading him correctly and that he would take the chance of happiness that was so close to him.

But she had never spoken a word. She was too wise to risk upsetting the delicate equilibrium of the situation.

Not everyone was so pleased by this development. Athene's parents exchanged cold-eyed glances and were now prepared to advance on John, determined not to let their chance slip.

John was looking around for Benedict, wondering why his friend was not there to congratulate him. But he seemed to have vanished.

He gave a signal to the musicians to resume the ball and music soared out overhead. The dancers began to swirl again. Drusilla, he was sorry to note, was again clasped too closely in the arms of another good-looking young man.

John realised that Arthur Scuggins was standing beside him. His eyes were fixed on Drusilla, who seemed suddenly to become aware of him and ran forward, leaving her partner stranded in the middle of the floor.

"I have a dance free now, Arthur," she said teasingly. "Isn't it lucky you are so patient."

"Yes, my dear," he said gravely. "I think it is much better that I waited."

He turned to John, looking pale and almost distraught.
"Your Grace – "

"John. Or Chesterton, if you must be formal."

"Chesterton, may I speak with you?"

"Of course, old fellow. What can I do for you?"

"It had been my intention to ask your permission to marry Drusilla."

"I grant that permission. I think she is a very lucky girl."

He gave a wan smile.

"I doubt if she would agree with you. In any case, I do not, now, intend to seek her hand."

Drusilla gave a little scream and her hands flew to her mouth.

"Don't tell me you have quarrelled over an evening's dancing?" John enquired.

"Not at all. It is merely that I have realised the hopelessness of my position."

"It is not hopeless. Drusilla has been intending to marry you these last two weeks. She told me so. Repeatedly."

"Yes, because she was afraid of being poor."

Arthur looked into Drusilla's face and his voice was very gentle.

"My dear, I mean no disrespect to you if I say that I know the chief attraction is my money. How could it be otherwise, when I am so much older than you and you have so much life and beauty?"

"I think you are a dashed good match for her," John insisted.

"I might have been, if you had not found a Rembrandt. But I know what it will be worth. Now you will have all the money you can possibly want. You can restore this place and Drusilla can take her rightful position in Society – a society that would never accept me."

He looked kindly at Drusilla.

"You don't need me now," he told her.

"You don't know that," Gina said quickly. "What about her feelings? What about love?"

He gave her a wry smile.

"You are surely not suggesting that Drusilla is in love with me?"

There was an awkward silence as each one of them remembered Drusilla's behaviour that evening.

"She is young," John said awkwardly. "A little flirting – I grant that it was improper – "

"No, it was not improper," Arthur insisted at once.

He turned back to Drusilla, standing there, her eyes full of horror, fixed on his face. Gently he took her hand.

"As you say, she is young and a little innocent flirting is no more than she is entitled to."

"But – I didn't mean it," Drusilla stammered.

"My dear girl, be young and enjoy yourself without an elderly husband around to spoil everything for you. The fault was mine for ever daring to intrude on your life."

He gave a little bow in John's direction.

"Chesterton, I withdraw my suit and I bid you all goodnight."

Everyone there was dismayed, but nobody knew how to stop this dignified man from doing what he had decided. He had a will of iron. That much was clear.

For a moment everyone in the little group was frozen as they watched Arthur Scuggins walk calmly away.

Then the air was rent by a terrible shriek.

"Arthur! *Wait*."

But he did not stop.

"Go after him," Gina said urgently.

Gathering up her skirts Drusilla sped across the floor and the dancers parted before her.

"Arthur!" she screamed.

"We had better follow," counselled Lady Evelyn worriedly. "She will need us to console her."

In the corridor outside they saw Drusilla catch up with Arthur and fling her arms about his neck.

"Don't go," she wept. "I love you."

"You are a child. You do not know what love means."

"I know that I love you," she cried. "I know I have been mean and horrible tonight – "

"No, my darling, you have just acted like a girl at her first dance."

"But it will never be my first dance again," she explained quickly, "so that will be all right, won't it?"

Even the troubled Arthur had to smile at this piece of disjointed logic.

"And I don't care about Society," she hurried on. "We will just entertain your friends, all the other grocers and – your friends and I can just flirt with them."

"You most certainly will not," he said sternly but beginning to smile.

"I will, I will, and I will make you very proud of me."

"I think you and Drusilla need to have a long talk," John intervened. "Just walking away from her is not the answer."

Arthur shook his head doubtfully.

"Please," Drusilla said, looking up tearfully into his face. "There is so much I want to say to you, Arthur dear."

"Go into the library," suggested Lady Evelyn. "I will have some refreshment sent to you."

Arthur threw her a look of gratitude and allowed himself to be drawn away by Drusilla, who held his hand tightly, as if fearful that he should escape.

"It's up to her, now," John said. "Now she has discovered the value of what she nearly lost, she will have to work to keep him."

"I think she will manage it," Lady Evelyn commented.

John nodded.

"I do hope so."

"But Mr. Scuggins was right in a way," Gina mused. "She could marry a title and live in Society now. And yet, here you are, trying to match her to a man who must seem no more than a tradesman to you."

John smiled ruefully.

"Maybe I know a little more now than I did earlier," he told her. "Drusilla would be lucky to have a man who loves her enough to put up with her feather-brained ways. And she seems dashed fond of him. They could be the perfect couple."

Gina smiled.

This was the man she loved.

Then her smile faded as she remembered that this was the man she was about to lose.

They were making their way back to the picture gallery, when they saw Athene's parents waiting for them in the doorway.

John groaned.

"Now, Your Grace, I will not be put off any longer," asserted Mr. Wicks-Henderson firmly.

"I was not aware that I was putting you off," John answered, trying to be pleasant. "I have merely been very distracted with so much happening."

"Yes, so I have seen. Now that you are rich again, I suppose you think you are above my daughter."

"I beg your pardon!"

"You know what I mean. I am talking about my Athene – where is the girl by the way? She ought to be here."

It dawned on John that he had not seen Athene for some time, but he could only be glad that she was not here to witness what was clearly going to be a very vulgar scene. Every time her father spoke, John was engulfed in heavy wine fumes.

"Shall we go aside to talk?" he asked, indicating the door to a small ante-room.

"Oh, yes, you would like to fob me off, wouldn't you? But I am staying here until you tell me that you are going to do the right thing by my girl."

"And may I ask what you consider *the right thing* to be?" John asked in a tone that was all the more dangerous for being quiet.

"As if I needed to say! She has lived under your roof all this time – "

"As the guest of my mother," John reminded him.

Gina, watching this scene with clenched fists, became aware that Pharaoh was at her elbow.

"I was asked to give you this," he murmured.

It was a pale blue envelope with her name written on it in Athene's hand writing. Frowning, she tore it open.

Athene's father raised his voice.

"My girl has spent all her time with you, riding over the countryside in full view of the world."

"If the world has been watching so closely," John said, "then the world will have noticed that we did not ride alone, but in company with this lady and a friend of mine."

"Fine talk, but everyone has seen you together and knows she has been staying here, and I say that the time has come for you to make an offer for her hand."

John drew a sharp breath.

Now it was placed before him starkly he knew that the thought of marriage to Athene was appalling. Her beauty could never make up for her infantile conversation and the total lack of any mental communion between them. And this would be true even if he was not in love with another woman.

But to marry Athene when he had discovered his perfect woman in Gina! Even if he could never marry his beloved, she would remain his ideal of perfection all his life and to be tied to another woman was unthinkable.

But, even as he dwelt on these thoughts, he wondered if what this man was saying might be true. Had he compromised Athene? Would he be obliged to marry her, even though it would mean a lifetime of misery for them both?

He closed his eyes, praying for a miracle to save him.

Once, it seemed long ago, Gina had promised him a miracle. But surely even Gina could not save him now.

"I am waiting, Your Grace," said Wicks-Henderson.

"Does Athene say I have compromised her?" John asked, playing for time.

"Yes, she does," put in Athene's mother quickly.

"Yet she chooses to absent herself from this conversation," John observed.

"Where is she?" Athene's mother snapped, looking around with her little sharp eyes. "Bring her here and then we'll see."

"I am afraid that will not be possible," Gina said slowly, her eyes on the letter she was holding.

"What do you mean, not possible?" Wicks-Henderson roared. "Where is she?"

"A long way away by now," Gina informed him. "This is a letter from her to me, explaining why she will not be returning."

She began to read,

"*Dear Gina,*

Do forgive me for doing this to you in the middle of the ball, but there was no other way.

Benedict and I are in love. It struck us both like a flash of lightning at the first moment and we have lived only for each other since ever then.

My parents will never consent to our marriage, so we have run away together. When you next see me I will be Mrs. Benedict Kenly.

Please give my apologies to the Duke. I never meant to mislead him, but he didn't really want to marry me anyway. He – "

Gina checked herself at this point, for the letter continued,

"He loves someone else and I think you know who. If you haven't guessed by now, then you must be very blind."

Omitting this passage, Gina hurried on to the final words.

"Your affectionate friend,

Athene."

There was a stunned silence before Athene's parents let out a joint roar and pounced, snatching the letter from Gina's hand.

"We'll get her back – "

"He's abducted our girl – "

"He won't get away with it – "

John hardly heard any of this. It was being borne on him, like a burst of music, that he had misunderstood Benedict's words. It was not Gina that he loved and who had said she loved him, but *Athene.*

And Gina?

Who did she love?

He turned to look and her and found her regarding him, a yearning look in her eyes. His heart began to beat strongly as he thought he understood that look. If only he was not mistaken.

If only –

"Your Grace will be hearing from me," Mr. Wicks-Henderson bawled. "If you had done your duty earlier this would not have happened."

"It would always have happened," John replied as if in a dream. "Your daughter is in love with Benedict – "

"In love? What has that got to do with it?"

"It has everything to do with it?" John said fiercely. "In fact, it is the only thing that matters. Athene is right. If you have found the one person in the world that you care about, then you should go through fire and ice to be with that person."

His eyes were on Gina as he spoke.

"It doesn't matter what else you have to give up," he added. "Give up the rest of the world and cling to that one person – if she will have you."

He saw by the faint smile in Gina's face that she had understood and his heart soared.

"And what does this bit mean?" Mr. Wicks-Henderson screamed, stabbing at the letter, "*he loves someone else – *"

"Give me that," John shouted in swift rage and snatched the letter from him.

He immediately returned it to Gina, although he longed to read the mysterious passage that she had omitted.

"Oho! I see," Athene's father sneered, looking from one to the other. "That's the way of it, is it?"

"Do not let me detain you," John told him in a frosty voice.

Mr. Wicks-Henderson snorted. His wife sniffed. But it was useless. They were defeated and they knew it. They were still frothing with rage as they departed and the ball began to break up.

Guests approached John to say their farewells. He played his part, smiled, and made the right remarks and all the time his mind was seething with questions.

Had he imagined Gina's reaction?

What would she say to him when they were alone?

Did she really love him?

After all his blind stupidity, would he be given a second chance?

At last most of the guests were gone and only those who were staying the night remained.

"Leave them to me," his mother told him. "Go to Gina."

"Mama – "

"It is what I hoped for, my dear boy. She is the perfect wife for you, I knew it from the first."

"You – ?"

"Why else do you think I invited her to stay? I was not going to take the chance of her escaping. You need her too much."

"I thought you wanted me to marry Athene."

"Goodness no! I knew she would bore you within five minutes. I thought the more you saw of her, the quicker you would become disillusioned. With Gina it was the opposite. I knew the more you saw of her, the more you would value her."

"And I did. But perhaps she won't have me, Mama."

"If she has any sense, she won't have you," agreed Lady Evelyn with spirit. Then she softened. "But I rely on her being too much in love to have any sense."

The picture gallery was almost empty. John could see Gina at the far end, concentrating on some flowers.

With sudden determination he marched towards her, seized her hand and whisked her out of the room.

The next moment she was in his arms.

It was the kiss they had both dreamed of and believed could never happen. John pressed her fervently against his heart, thanking Heaven for his miracle.

He kissed her fiercely, passionately, rejoicing as he felt her sweet response.

Inspired, he kissed her again, trying to tell her, without words, all the feelings that were in his heart.

"I thought you loved Benedict," he said at last.

"And I thought you loved Athene."

"What do I care for her? I wish Benedict every happiness, but she could never suit me. I think I must have loved you from the first moment, but you convinced me that I had no hope."

"I – ?"

"You insisted that I needed an heiress, but you never told me that you were one, so I took that as a rejection. You little witch! Why did you send for Athene?"

"But I never did, I told you. It was just a coincidence her turning up like that."

"After what you said about knowing an heiress?"

Her smile turned his heart over.

"There was no heiress – unless, perhaps, I meant myself. I wanted to know what you would say to the prospect. And I also wanted you to love me, but I could not bear to think that my money was an attraction, so I pretended not to have any. I should have trusted you better."

"But I don't need an heiress now," he said, "so you can believe me when I say that it is love and love alone that makes me beg you to be my wife."

She searched his face longingly.

"Do you really love me, my darling? Is it possible?"

"It is not possible for me to love anyone else. I was a fool, Gina, but I am a fool no longer. Tell me that it isn't too late."

"It isn't too late," she whispered. "We found each other, as I believe we were always meant to do."

He drew her against him again for a kiss that was full of tenderness and joy.

When at last he released his lips, he said in a shaking

voice,

"My mother tells me that she always wanted this. She will be delighted to have you as a daughter-in-law."

"Let us go and share our happiness with her, quickly," Gina suggested.

They hurried in search of Lady Evelyn, but could find no trace of her. They hunted through several rooms, until at last they approached the library.

"Perhaps she has gone to bed," John observed. "I hope not, because I don't want to wait until morning to – Mama!"

As he spoke, John was opening the door, half turning to speak over his shoulder and then looking back into the library. And what he saw there brought him to a sudden halt.

"Mama!" he repeated.

The couple in the room sprang apart. On Lady Evelyn's face was a rosy blush that made her seem much younger than her years. And as she looked at the man with her and took his hand, she wore a look of blinding happiness.

"Ambrose!" John said slowly. "Mama – "

"Oh, darling, don't be angry with me," Lady Evelyn said. "I couldn't help it. Truly I couldn't."

As she spoke she looked at Ambrose again and John drew in his breath at that look. Like all the young, he had not thought of his mother as a woman who could be in love. But there was no doubting the adoration in the gaze she turned on her beloved.

"It is all my fault," Ambrose explained hastily. "I have loved Lady Evelyn for years, ever since I came here to pay a respectful visit to the late Duke. In fact, that was why I offered myself to him as a secretary." He turned worshipful eyes on John's Mama. "It was a chance to be near – her."

"Oh, I think it's so lovely," Gina sighed.

"But Gina," John murmured, aghast, "this is my mother."

"Well, she is a free agent. She is a widow. If she

wants to love again, that's nobody's business but hers."

"But – Papa – "

"I loved your father devotedly while he was alive," Lady Evelyn said. "But now that I am alone – cannot you try to understand?"

"I hope I do not need to say that my attentions have been respectful," Ambrose began.

"There wasn't anything very respectful about the way you were kissing my mother just then," John pointed out.

Lady Evelyn giggled,

"There wasn't, was there?"

"Mama!"

"Oh, don't be so stuffy, John dear! Really, the young can be so conventional. Gina, I rely on you to improve him."

"I will do my best ma'am, but it will be hard because I think he is nearly perfect as he is."

"Of course, I realise that I am far below Lady Evelyn in station," Ambrose said.

"And I am just a little older than you," Lady Evelyn sighed.

"I don't believe it," Ambrose declared gallantly. "You are as young as springtime."

John pulled himself together. He was a good son and a kind hearted young man and his mother's happiness was important to him.

"Look, old fellow," he said, "don't worry about anything. If you are trying to ask me for my mother's hand in marriage, I grant it."

His Mama gave a gasp of indignation.

"*I* haven't granted it yet."

"Well, grant it then," her son advised her.

"But he has not asked me," she replied in high dudgeon. "A lady likes to be proposed to properly."

"I doubt if he will propose," John said airily. "He is

too conscious of being a poor relation and other things that don't matter. So if you just say 'yes' that will save him the trouble."

John clapped Ambrose on the shoulder and kissed his mother's cheek.

"Bless you my children," he intoned.

Then he took Gina's hand and whisked her out of the room. The last glimpse he saw as he closed the door was Ambrose going down on one knee.

Safe outside the door John and Gina leaned against the wall and collapsed with laughter.

"Oh, dear, oh, dear!" Gina gasped. "Why are we laughing? It is so beautiful."

"Yes, it's beautiful, but it's also crazy," John choked. "Mama isn't 'just a little older' than Ambrose. She is ten years older than Ambrose."

"Well, of course he knows that," Gina pointed out. "The details of a Ducal family are no secret. He knows her age, but he will pretend not to if it makes her happy."

"If he doesn't make her happy, I will have his hide," John observed.

"I am so glad you made it easy for them," Gina sighed. "That was a very kind thing you just did."

"It's just that I want the entire world to be as happy as I am," John said, taking her into his arms again.

"As happy as we are," Gina added.

"I will devote my life to making you happy," he told her seriously. "If only you will say that you love me, Gina."

"I love you with my whole heart and soul and I always will."

"Your love is all I want. And now that I have it, I have the miracle you once promised me. And I know that there will be a new miracle every day for the rest of our lives."